BLUE PLATE SPECIAL

A Table for Two Novella

LAYLA REYNE

Blue Plate Special

Copyright © 2023 by Layla Reyne

E-Book ISBN: 979-8-9869229-1-1

Print ISBN: 979-8-9869229-5-9

Cover Design: Cate Ashwood Designs; Editing: Susie Selva; Proofreading: Lori Parks

Content Warnings: Explicit sex including mild kink; explicit language; on-page instances and discussion of homophobia; on-page flashbacks and discussion of past abuse by a parent; off-page death of a parent.

About This Book

An order you can't resist...

Ingredients:
One thirty-something chef hiding from his past behind a
diner counter.
One silver fox venture capitalist who left the big city to
save his health and heart.
A chance meeting with his son's former best friend who's
all grown up and exudes the kind of quiet, commanding
presence he craves.

Directions:
Toss ingredients into a small-town Southern skillet with a
heaping dash of drama.
Turn up the heat with orders in the bedroom for a sizzling
good sear but mind the clock.
Don't let things get too hot or feelings might stick... or
someone might get burned.

Cook to the perfect temp—love—for a juicy, delicious
forever.

*Savor this steamy age-gap M/M romance novella while
noshing on your favorite guilty pleasure.*

For every chef, home and professional, who poured their heart and soul into making dishes that made my heart and soul happy.

Prologue

Thirteen Years Ago

Hudson shifted in the passenger seat of his best friend's Corvette, every motion a lick of fire across his back, and at the speed Tyler was pushing the sports car, Hudson's back was an inferno. He could scoot back in the seat for more stability, but the last thing he wanted to do was get blood all over Ty's new car. So he swayed with every lane change and sudden turn, gritting his teeth against the searing pain—too used to it and not used to it at all.

There had been other cuts and bruises, too many to count, but he'd never feared for his life before tonight. He'd also never had someone else take a blow for him or had to fear for that person's life.

His best friend's life.

Wincing, Hudson glanced at Ty behind the wheel, his blue eyes fixed on the road out of the city; red hair mussed by the girl he'd brought home from the regatta party; the welt on the outside of his shoulder an angry red against his pale skin. They'd left their building in such a hurry neither of them had grabbed their coats. Ty had shoved a T-shirt in Hudson's hands, a dark one by some miracle, and that's all there had been time for.

"I'm sorry," Hudson mumbled, voice croaky from the day's earlier shouting, both at the regatta and at home. "He wasn't supposed to find out."

Ty's reply was swift and full of rage. "You, Hudson Selby, have nothing to be sorry for." He channeled that rage into his foot on the gas. "This was *his* doing, not *yours*. And he was beating you before he found out you were gay, wasn't he?" At Hudson's nod, Ty drove even faster. "It has to end."

"I know." Hudson had thought he could make it two more years. He had an escape plan: graduate, turn twenty-two a month later, access the trust fund his late mother had left him, move across the country, and go to culinary school in Napa. But after tonight, he wasn't sure he'd survive staying two more years.

Silence reigned for the next half hour, Hudson only breaking it when Ty exited onto the Long Island Expressway. "We're going to the Hamptons?"

"My parents are there for the weekend."

"That's not—"

"They'll know what to do."

"But what if they call him?" Hudson's body tensed, and his voice rose before it cracked, the sudden shift, the aggravation of tattered skin and aching muscles, tossing him back into the lake of fire. When he spoke again, it was so weak, so gravelly, he could barely hear himself over the rumble of the 'Vette's tires. "What if they tell him to come get me?"

Blue eyes cut his direction, daybreak in the dark night. "You know my parents. They won't call him."

Hudson shifted his foot, angling for stability, and immediately regretted it, a hiss escaping his lips. Adrenaline had pushed the sprained ankle to the back of his mind during their mad dash out of the building but not any longer.

"You can sit back," Ty said.

"I'm not fucking up your 'Vette. I've fucked up enough tonight."

"*You* didn't fuck up anything, and I mean it, you'll be safe out here. There's a reason he's never vacationed with us, why his interactions with Mom and Dad are polite but not friendly." Despite living across the hall from each other for fifteen years. Despite Hudson and Tyler being best friends since the day they'd met. Hudson had always wondered but never questioned, never wanting to risk losing his safe haven.

Hudson bit back any further arguments, any further sound, until an hour later when Ty hurtled the 'Vette up the drive of the Rosins' second home, slicing between the vehicles parallel parked on either side of the long driveway. Bugatti, Ferrari, Porsche, none of them under six figures. "What are all these cars doing here?"

"It's one of my parents' parties. We'll slip in the back, and I'll go get them. They'll have a doctor here."

Why? But more pressing, "No! Just take me to a hotel or something."

"At midnight? Cut up like you are?" Ty swung the car around the horseshoe at the end of the drive then under an arch that led to a second parking area in front of the detached garage at the side of the house. "If we do that," Ty continued, "someone *will* call the cops."

Tyler was right. *Fuck,* he was right.

Hudson checked the frustrated punch he wanted to hurl at the dashboard. Not fair to the 'Vette, not fair to Ty, and not fair to his own aching body. The motion would surely make him scream in agony. "I gotta get outta here."

Car parked, Ty angled toward him and gently clasped his shoulder. "You gotta get seen to first, then we can think about what's next."

We.

Best friends forever. The saying was trite, but that's how Hudson felt about Tyler down to his bones. And Ty felt the same about him; his actions tonight proved it. He'd risked his own safety to rescue Hudson. Not a risk Hudson could let him take again. The world would be a much darker place without Tyler Rosin in it. Ty deserved to succeed at life and as a restaurateur. To find the woman of his dreams and produce an army of ginger-haired munchkins while building his culinary empire. He didn't deserve an albatross around his neck who would hold him back and endanger his life.

"Hey, Hud," Ty said from his other side, crouched in the open passenger door. When had he gotten out of the car? When had he circled to Hudson's side and opened the door? "Where'd you go?"

"Away."

Sadness streaked like a bullet across Ty's baby blues. He knew this only ended one way. He knew about the escape plan; he knew it had been irrevocably accelerated. He squeezed Hudson's knee. "Just stay with me a little longer."

Hudson nodded and let Ty help him out of the car. They shuffled to the mudroom door, Ty's arm slung low around his waist, steadiness that buffered each painful step, agony radiating from Hudson's right ankle to his leg, his hip, his back, his neck.

Ocean of fire didn't come close.

Letting them in with his key, Ty guided Hudson through the mudroom and into the service kitchen. The island was covered with decimated canapés and hors d'oeuvre trays, dirty plates and glasses were stacked next to the sink, and empty wine bottles were piled in the recycling bin. Typical Rosin party.

They were rounding the end of the prep table, headed for the stools on the other side, when the door to the main kitchen opened, a server balancing a tray of empty glasses. Surprised, she bobbled the tray and fell back against the door, unintentionally opening it wider.

Hudson saw straight through to the great room.

This wasn't just *any* party, and it definitely wasn't like the typical parties the Rosins threw on the Upper East Side.

Mrs. Rosin, her long dark curls uncharacteristically

loose, stood behind a chair, her breasts spilling out of a leather bustier, her arms draped over the shoulders of a naked man reclined in a chair, writhing as she pinched his pierced nipples. Hudson didn't recognize him. But the man on his knees between the stranger's spread legs, dressed only in black mesh briefs and sucking the other man's cock, had a strikingly familiar frame and a shock of ginger hair.

The same color as Hudson's best friend.

Mrs. Rosin's gaze shot up, drawn by the commotion. Her dark eyes widened as they landed on Tyler and Hudson. Her lips moved, then the man on his knees straightened and glanced over his shoulder.

Hudson's best friend's father stared back at them, his freckled cheeks flushed and his toned, hairy chest heaving, his abs rippling and the mesh briefs riding higher on his firm round ass. For a second, Hudson forgot all about the shooting pain in his ankle, the torn-open flesh on his back, and the throb in his neck where a boot had been pressed.

Mr. Rosin was fucking gorgeous.

And queer?

Tyler's earlier words came back to him. *"You'll be safe out here."*

For the first time that night, Hudson believed maybe he would be. Relief crashed through him, and fast on its heels followed the pain he'd momentarily forgotten. Finally safe, Hudson let it take him.

Chapter One

Noah slid a tray of cinnamon rolls into the baking oven, then wiped his sticky hands on his dirtier than dirty *Respect the Beard* apron. On the other side of the prep table, Jordan pitched his much more respectable, though no less dirty, Blue Plate-branded apron into the under-counter basket. "First class this morning?" Noah asked.

"First of the last." The HU senior grinned. "Mostly just business school prereqs and working on my honors thesis at this point."

"Better get going, then." Finance classes were in Paxton Hall at the opposite end of Hanover University's campus from where Blue Plate was next to Pearl's on Main Street. "Thanks for the hustle today."

"Always. Felt good to have a crowd again." Jordan smiled wider as he slung his backpack over his shoulder. "Felt *real good* to get out of the office and back in here." He'd split his time over the summer between the kitchen and working in the office with Candice, learning how the business part of the operation worked. But first and foremost, the kid loved to cook. "Do it again tomorrow!" he said with a slap to the prep table on his way out the door. In his wake, Noah peeked out the oculus window, checking to see how much of the crowd remained. Several booths were occupied, most of the tables by the front windows, and all the counter stools. But there was no line at the take-out register, and there were no tickets waiting on the kitchen display system.

A relative slowdown, at least until the lunch rush began at the end of the next class period. The first Monday of fall semester was no joke. They'd slung out more plates that morning than they had the past few months. And what a bountiful bunch of dishes they'd been, the late summer giving them so much to work with, like today's blue plate special, a farmers' market frittata—farm-fresh eggs, heirloom tomatoes, and herbs with a side of dandelion greens dressed in a summer citrus vinaigrette. The rest of the menu didn't stray far from café and diner favorites, but even those Noah liked to spruce up. French toast with mixed berries, scratch-made biscuits with seasonal jams, sheep's milk yogurt and homemade granola, an omelet with colorful heirloom tomato slices.

Noah eyed the half crate of tomatoes he had left and calculated portions in his head. Just enough for tomato flatbreads for tomorrow. Overnight marinated mozzarella would add a nice touch. He was running through other blue plate ideas for the week, head in a fridge checking for ingredients, when the kitchen door swung open again. He didn't have to look to know who the easygoing tread and slap of flip-flops belonged to.

Three years ago, Candice had taken a chance on him, despite his checkered job history. He didn't stay in one place more than a few years—safer that way. Not every employer was willing to overlook the long string of jobs and addresses, despite his good references. Candice hadn't had time to question. She'd just lost her cook, a week before fall semester began, and she was desperate. His chili recipe was convincing enough. Hands down, she'd been the best boss he'd ever worked for, letting him stretch his wings and the diner budget with more farm-to-table items. The diner's popularity had also grown as a result, making it one of the handful of local places that held its own against the national chains moving into town. He hoped Candice and Jordan would carry on the trend after he left. Which he needed to do. Soon. He'd already stayed in Hanover too long, and he was getting too comfortable.

Comfortable gave the past time to catch up.

"Everything okay in there?" Candice asked from behind him.

"Yeah, all good," he said, shaking off the phantom sensation of a foot pressed against his neck. "Just putting together the specials for the week." He closed the fridge and leaned back against the door, enjoying the cool stainless steel through his thin T-shirt. "I'm thinking heirloom tomato flatbreads tomorrow, breakfast sandwiches with tomato and avocado on Wednesday, and summer squash casserole on Thursday." He divvied up his specials between breakfast and lunch. The early folks would get a treat some days, the lunch crowd others. "Chili, as usual, on Friday, then playing the weekend by ear depending on the crowd and produce."

Candice picked up a Cherokee Purple tomato. "I'm gonna be sad when these babies disappear. They've been so good this year, and the dishes you make with them..." She gestured a chef's kiss, and Noah chuckled.

He slipped the tomato from her hand and tugged her toward the dry-goods pantry. He opened the cool dark cabinet where he kept his pickling vegetables now together with a dozen jars of canned tomatoes. "I know it's not the same, but when the craving hits..."

Her answering smile didn't quite reach her light brown eyes. She was smart; she'd done the math. He'd be gone when the craving hit. She hid her dimmed grin in a sideways hug. "You, Noah Becker, are the best chance I ever took."

And driving thirty miles farther south to answer one want ad in Hanover versus several in Wilmington had been the best chance he'd ever taken. He saved them both the awkwardness of admitting his inevitable absence and joked instead, "I won't tell your wife you said that."

Tension cut, they were both still laughing when the KDS pinged, a new order incoming. "You need help back here?" Candice asked.

"Nah, Alicia will be here in twenty. I'm set until then."

"Okay, just holler if that changes."

"Will do." He waited for her to exit before snagging the order off the KDS.

Blue plate special, side of toast, double jam.

Abel Champion, if Noah had to guess. The former chief of police had a serious sweet tooth. The table number confirmed it, always the corner booth. What would Abel think about his homemade strawberry balsamic spread? And who did the second KDS ticket tagged to Abel's table belong to? His wife, Rachel, would be at work at this hour. Noah started toward the door, aiming to take a peek, and nearly collided with Holly as she barreled into the kitchen and swooned in the direction of the prep table. Used to her theatrics, Noah saved a tumbling cutting board with one hand and caught a flying strawberry with the other, popping the latter into his mouth. "Do I need to get the smelling salts?"

"Maybe," she heaved. "Or maybe just some water."

Laughing, Noah tossed the cutting board into the sink and fetched a bottle of water out of the fridge. There really was no better person to wait tables at Blue Plate than Holly, a retired dental hygienist who relished the new gig where people actually talked *with* her. She made everyone who walked through the diner's doors feel welcome, like they were the center of her attention, which they totally were. Holly was an incorrigible gossip, and she took in every tidbit someone shared and embellished like a pro. Noah handed her the bottle. "Who's got you swooning? Wait, let me guess... A hot new doctor in town just off her shift? Or maybe the new English lit professor?"

"No one will ever be as hot as Trevor Caldwell."

"Preach," he conceded. "So it's a professor?"

She nodded as she cracked open the water bottle. "The chief's friend. I can't remember his name. Was too busy trying not to drool." She downed half the water. "Abel said they went to school together. He's a visiting professor at the business school."

If he was a classmate of Abel's... "Silver fox?"

"*Ginger* fox," she said with a wicked grin. "There's some silver in there, but you wouldn't know it for that body." She fanned herself, and Noah laughed out loud. "I call dibs, but if Professor Sexy is into men, you need to get on that." She drained the rest of the water and tossed the bottle into the recycling bin. "And I mean that in *all* the senses of the word." Grinning, she batted her long fake lashes at him then practically skipped out the door.

On a fact-slash-matchmaking mission, God help them all.

Still chuckling, Noah returned to the task at hand, scrolling the rest of the way down to the second order on the ticket for Abel's table.

Everything bagel, toasted well. Lox, cream cheese, red onion. No capers.

His laughter died as a ghost skittered up his spine, memories of burnt bagels and salty mistakes tickling his senses. Another followed as a pronounced New York accent drifted through the swinging door. He was used to his own diminished accent, but whenever he heard a thicker, crisper one, he struggled not to flee into the nearest bathroom and hyperventilate, unable to stop the horror reel from playing in his mind.

"My son, the fag." The slap *of a belt. "Kicked off crew because he couldn't keep his dick in his pants." Another* slap. *"It was bad enough you were the fucking cox. A*

fucking Lion legacy too small to do anything more. How am I going to explain this to people?"

He forced words through his compressed windpipe. "I don't need to row to be a chef."

"A what?"

Compressed more. "I want to cook."

"I'm not paying fifty grand a year for you to fucking cook." Another slap, accompanied by an unbearable sting, his skin splitting open. "Or to stick your dick in your team-mate's ass. I will make a real Selby man out of you if it's the last goddamn thing I do."

Was today the day his past caught up with him? Because he'd gotten too comfortable here, joking with Holly, mentoring Jordan, and making Candice happy? He eyed the still-swinging door. He could peek through the window to confirm his worst nightmare had come true... or to confirm he was hearing things and jumping to all the wrong conclusions. Or he could run to the bathroom and hyperventilate like his insides were screaming at him to do. Or he could suck it up and fill the damn order like he'd done countless other times.

He washed his hands and got to work. Ten minutes later, he sent the order ready notice to Holly, who returned to the kitchen with a different directive. "Bring that out yourself. Abel wants to sing your praises to Professor Sexy."

"That's not—"

Holly vanished before he could finish his protest. No help for it if he wanted his food served hot. He wiped his hands on the towel over his shoulder, then yanked it off and hooked it around the laces of his apron.

He was halfway to the corner booth when the man across from Abel shifted enough for Noah to glimpse his profile. Noah skidded to a halt, the ghosts from earlier materializing—only in a slightly different direction than he'd anticipated, but *fuck*, he should have guessed given what Holly had said.

Abel spotted him, his deep voice booming the length of the diner. "Noah, get over here. I wanna introduce you."

The other man at Abel's table rotated the rest of the way around, and bright blue eyes stared back at Noah from under a headful of hair that had faded from bright red to an attractive copper shot through with silvery white.

Ginger fox indeed.

There was a split second where Noah thought maybe he had escaped—he looked nothing like his old self—but then Mr. Rosin's eyes flared with recognition. "Hudson, is that you?"

"I'm sorry, you must have me confused with someone else." Noah set the plates on the table. "Please enjoy your food."

"Noah, wait!" Abel called after him.

Noah didn't look back. He put one foot in front of the other as fast as he could short of a run, ignoring the memories unspooling in his head and fleeing from the part of his past that had found him in the present.

Scared to death the rest of his past—the awful part— wasn't far behind.

Chapter Two

"Why'd you call him Hudson?" Abel asked quietly, seeming to understand discretion was advised. Or maybe that was just the former detective in him. In which case, Ezra needed to handle this with equal discretion. He did not want to raise suspicions that would reflect poorly on Hudson.

"I should go apologize," Ezra said, likewise speaking low as he stood from the booth. "Is there a back door to the kitchen?" He figured that for Hudson's exit but needed a less scene-causing path to it.

Abel nodded. "Follow the walkway around the side of the building to the gravel lot out back."

Ezra didn't waste another second, wanting to confirm what his eyes, what the fluttering in his chest—the good kind—had told him. Hudson Selby was there, in Hanover, and had just served him breakfast. Ezra also knew, with absolute certainty, that Hudson Selby would go on the run again if Ezra didn't stop him. He cleared the back corner of the building and caught sight of Hudson halfway across the gravel parking lot.

And nearly tripped as he second-guessed himself.

At twenty, Hudson had rowed crew for Columbia, had rowed for most of his life, same as Ezra's son, but unlike Tyler, Hudson had been relatively small in stature. A natural at the cox position. But the man striding across the parking lot toward a truck parked in the far corner was massive. Several inches taller than Ezra with broad shoulders, biceps that tested the limits of his T-shirt, thighs that tested the limits of his jeans, and a mohawk of brown hair that was tied in a stub at the crown of his otherwise shaved head.

Maybe he was wrong. Maybe it wasn't Hudson Selby. But if it was...

"Hudson, wait!"

The man's steps faltered. It *was* him. But it wasn't. What did Abel say his name was? *Oy*. As if Ezra could forget it—his own son's middle name—but he was still so stunned. "I mean, Noah," he said, and Hudson started walking faster again. "Please, Noah, wait!"

Hudson froze with his hand on the truck door.

"I'm sorry." Ezra approached slowly, shuffling his loafers on the gravel so Hudson would hear exactly where he was, would know Ezra wasn't going to rush him. "I shouldn't have called you Hudson."

He turned and rested back against the truck, eyes downcast. "Look, Mr. Rosin—"

Ezra held out a hand, in Hud—Noah's—line of sight.

"I'm Ezra," he said, introducing himself as he would to a stranger, as the man before him was or at the very least wanted to be. And Ezra needed to keep him talking, needed to keep him there. "I like your apron."

The bright yellow thing with its funny saying—especially on a man with a more than respectable beard—would have made him laugh out loud under any other circumstances.

Nothing about it seemed to make Noah laugh in the moment. Cursing, he yanked it off and chucked it into the truck bed. "It's silly."

"That's not a bad thing. Finding humor in one's work is something a lot of people could benefit from."

Gray eyes flickered up, then closed. The brief glance was startling. Their color had always been unusual, but in a younger, rounder face with a pronounced nose and shaggy brown hair, they'd not been Hudson's most dominant feature. Now, though, with his face long and lean, the thick brown beard making it appear even more so, his nose better proportioned, and his eyes deep-set on either side of it, the stormy grays were a haunting focal point. They moved behind Hudson's closed lids, his chest heaving at a similarly rapid pace.

"Just breathe, Hud—" *Oy*, again. "Noah," he corrected himself.

A couple slower breaths later, Noah lifted his gaze. "I'm sorry. I'm surprised is all. To see you here."

"Are you okay?"

"Yeah."

Ezra made a sweeping gesture. "And in the larger sense?"

Noah chuckled, and his shoulders relaxed a notch. "Yeah, that too."

"Abel tells me you're quite the chef."

"Cook."

"Semantics," Ezra said with a flick of his hand. He talked with them a lot. Occupational hazard. He hoped it worked in the classroom as well as it had in the boardroom.

"You sound like Mrs. R." As soon as the words were out, tension rushed back in, Noah's shoulders climbing. "Is she here too?"

Ezra moved to step forward, to reach out and lay a hand on Noah's arm, but when the other man flinched, Ezra retreated. "No, just me." He shoved his hands into his pockets. Safer there. "Al and I divorced last year."

Tension vanished on a shocked gasp. "But you two... I thought..." His brow crinkled. "You two were always so happy, so in love." He averted his gaze again, and red streaked across his cheekbones. "Clearly, I didn't know *everything*." Ten to one he was recalling the position he'd found them in when he and Tyler had arrived at that party in the Hamptons thirteen years ago.

The last night any of them had seen Hudson Selby.

Until today.

"*That* had nothing to do with the divorce," Ezra said. "I met Al at a party like the one you walked in on. I still love her, she's my best friend, but she needed to do something else with her life, and I needed to do something else with mine."

Ezra's answer did nothing to flatten the divot between Noah's brows. "So you came here?"

"For the fall, to teach a couple business school classes. Abel's doing. He's an old friend. I bought a winery in Sonoma, but I don't take possession until January. Had some time to kill." And he was trying not to kill himself too.

"Sonoma? A winery?" Noah couldn't hide the curiosity and wistfulness in his voice. If he was anywhere near as good a cook as Abel had let on, Wine Country would hold a certain culinary mystique, same as it did for Ezra as a foodie.

"I know, typical bored venture capitalist. Vineyards or restaurants. Ty already claimed the latter, so I had to take the former." Ezra rolled his eyes at himself, then laid a hand over his heart, remembering the several reasons he'd upended his life. "I'm way in over my head, but I needed a change, and I wanted to be near Ty and his family."

Noah stepped forward, the divot disappearing and his lips curving up, his whole face brightening. *There* was the young man Ezra knew, always wanting the best for his friend. "Ty got married? He has kids?"

"To another redhead." He withdrew his phone, opened the photo app, and scrolled to the picture from Cape Cod earlier that spring. "They have two ginger babies, Molly and Michael."

Noah took the phone and affection flooded his features, smoothing over the rough edges. "Good," he said softly. "I'm happy for him." He looked another moment, then offered the phone back.

"I'm sure he'd want to—"

Noah snatched the phone back out of Ezra's reach. "No, please." All the rough edges prickled again. "You can't—"

Ezra raised both hands, palms out. "I won't say anything if you don't want me to."

Noah bit his bottom lip and curled his hand around the phone. "I don't want to risk that." He shoved the phone back at Ezra. "I don't want to risk any of you." He'd said something similar that night thirteen years ago.

"We need to call the police," Ezra had said. Wrapped in a robe, he sat beside a similarly robed Al on the window ledge in the study. Hudson sat beside Tyler on the leather chaise, the standby doctor for the party treating their wounds. Tyler's were minor, but Hudson's... Ezra could barely look at the cuts on the poor boy's back, his bandaged ankle, or the bruise darkening the back of his neck without feeling nauseous.

"You can't." Hudson's red-rimmed eyes shot to his. "When Ty said he was getting me out of there..." His gaze strayed to the bruise blooming on Tyler's arm. "He threatened..." He gulped. "I don't want him coming after any of you. I need to go."

"Go where?"

"I don't know. Away. Some place he's not."

Ezra started to object, but Ty cut him off. "This was always the plan. Just a couple years early."

The nausea rose higher, bile stinging the back of Ezra's throat. "How long has this been going on?" he asked

Hudson. "How long have you known?" he demanded of his son.

Neither Ty nor Hudson answered, and Ezra moved to push off the ledge. Al held him in place by the elbow. "Let it go, hon."

He raked a hand through his hair instead. Fuck, how had they missed it? How had they lived across the hall for fifteen years and never realized? How had they never seen or heard? Fuck!

When the doctor finished and exited, Al pushed off the window. "Get a couple stacks from the safe," she ordered Ezra.

Still half in sub space to her Domme, and more than half used to following her orders when it came to their family too, he crossed the room to Al's favorite landscape photo—a black and white of a rain-soaked Central Park. He swung the framed picture aside, opened the wall safe behind it, and removed two stacks of bills.

Beside him, Al retrieved her bulging business card case from the lower desk drawer, flipped through the collection, and withdrew one from the middle. She held out her hand for the stacks, stepped out from behind the desk, and crossed the room to Hudson, who was slumped against Tyler's side. She knelt in front of him and gently laid a hand on his knee. "Ezra will get dressed and take you to whatever drop-off point you want. Bus station, Grand Central, JFK, you name it." She handed him the card first. "Call this attorney. Tell him Annaliese Rosin referred you. He specializes in emancipating LGBTQ youths from abusive parents. I've worked several pro bono cases with him."

"But I'm over eighteen."

"And without access to your trust fund yet."

He lowered his gaze.

"He'll help you get it, and more importantly, he'll make sure your father never finds you again. None of us will, unless you want us to, and that's your choice." She handed him the stacks of bills. "Use this to get on your feet, wherever you end up, and go to culinary school. Fuck your father. I've seen you cook and tasted your talent. It's too good to waste."

Ezra wondered if Noah had gone to culinary school, if that was part of the talent Abel was tasting or if it was more of that innate talent Ezra had been privileged to experience whenever a younger Hudson would cook for them. But given the eggshells they were already walking on, Ezra decided against bringing up another potentially painful subject. And besides, there was another path to his answer.

He took back the phone and reversed a step, giving Noah space and safety, hoping it was enough for the ask he wanted to make. "Do you mind if I come into Blue Plate from time to time? The location is convenient, and I'd like to try this food of yours Abel raves about."

A plea for Noah to stay, in so many words.

"I can't stop you."

"But I can respect your wishes. To not tell Ty and Al you're here and to not visit Blue Plate if that's what you want. Whatever you need, Noah. That's all we've ever tried to give you."

Noah lowered his gaze again. "I know and thank you. I'm sorry I didn't write or call or say thank you before."

"You didn't have to. You never had to." The familiar sting of bile crept up his throat. "I'm sorry we didn't do more sooner."

Noah inhaled deep, then straightened and righted his gaze. The resolve in his steely eyes checked Ezra's rising guilt and offered an ounce of hope. His words offered more. "You're welcome at Blue Plate anytime."

Chapter Three

Teaching was *not* like being in the boardroom. Granted, both Ezra's classes were for upperclassmen—one on joint venture deals, the other on negotiation—but he was so used to dealing with experienced parties across the table that taking the time to slow down, to explain the inner workings of a deal in plain English without thirty-plus years of professional shorthand, was challenging. But beneficial. He needed the reality check—a forced break from the rat race mentality that pervaded New York City deal-making —before tackling his new role as winery owner. His hand-picked winemaker had already warned him he'd need to learn to channel that New York energy and to make Wine Country deals in a more constructive, patient way.

At first, he'd balked when Abel had mentioned the position at HU, but his old friend had been right. He needed a period to downshift, and what better place to do that than in Hanover. It was like the Hamptons but without the glitz and pretentiousness, cozier and down to earth, with a beachy college-town vibe. He'd been born and raised in New York City. He'd never lived in a place like this. And he welcomed the chance to catch up on all the deep-sea fishing he'd been "too busy" to join Abel for over the years.

Years he might have discovered Hud—Noah. He had no idea how long Noah had been in Hanover, how long he'd been at Blue Plate, or how long he'd been cooking professionally. A while if Ezra had to guess. His cooking was everything Abel had promised. He'd planned to commend Noah, but after back-to-back classes and a Friday departmental meeting, it was after three before he made it to the diner only to learn Noah was gone for the day.

He pretended not to be disappointed as he drank his cavity-sweet iced tea and ate his pastrami on rye. It was delicious—the homemade slaw creamy and tangy against the rich, peppery beef and buttery grilled toast—but it didn't pack the same sort of surprise as the other dishes of Noah's he'd tried that week. Noah's culinary style was refined yet approachable, even if the chef was not. He rarely came out of the kitchen, and Ezra worried that absence was because of him.

"Is Noah usually off on Fridays?" he asked Holly as she refilled his tea.

"Sundays. He knocks off early on Fridays sometimes, if the crowd ain't too bad." She gave him a knowing smile. "Does someone have a crush on our cook?"

Ezra sputtered, not knowing what to do with such an absurd suggestion. This was Hud— no, it was Noah. He was a different person. Older, taller, broader. Attractively built and handsome in a way anyone would notice. But underneath all that sculpted bulk, he was still the same kid whose scraped knees Ezra had bandaged, who'd been attached at the hip to Ezra's son, who'd built sandcastles with them on vacation, and who'd cooked them breakfast anytime he'd slept over. Ezra had realized too late that those meals had been thank-you notes, tasty morsels of gratitude in exchange for nights of peace and safety. Ezra should have realized sooner what had been going on.

As if sensing his darkening mood, Holly poked his shoulder. She tossed her gray curls and batted her lashes. "I'm not personality enough?"

"You're wonderful." Tension easing on a grin, he navigated toward an answer to his earlier mental question. "You run a tight ship out here, mostly by yourself, it seems."

He gestured around them at the diner's inviting interior—white tile walls with a blue tile border, matching blue booths, seat covers, and bar stools, shiny chrome tables and a matching counter. Bright, clean, and one hundred percent small-town diner.

"Why thank you," Holly preened. "We've got a few more folks who work the morning shifts when we're busiest. Alicia's out here some too. And Candice, when she escapes the office."

"Average height, brunette bob, green eyes?" Ezra recalled seeing her yesterday flitting between tables.

Holly nodded. "She's the owner. Only one who spends more time here than Noah."

Ezra got that. He'd run his own venture capital firm for decades and, for better or worse, he'd been an incurable workaholic.

"Candice likes gossip almost as much as I do," Holly added with a wink. "I'll be sure to tell her you asked about our boy."

Ezra ignored the heat that hit his cheeks and aimed for the too-good-to-pass-up opening. "Noah stays in the back mostly?"

"Prefers to let the food speak for itself." She dropped off his check and headed back to the kitchen, poorly muffling a giggle.

Ezra likewise poorly muffled his sigh of relief. Noah's food did speak for itself and the cook. *Loudly.* Especially yesterday's squash casserole, which Ezra couldn't get out of his head. So much so that he stopped by the market on his way home for the ingredients to recreate it.

He was bent over, chasing a renegade squash that had rolled to the back of his trunk, when someone whistled from across the apartment complex parking lot. At him? Or at the car? Straightening and rotating, he found Noah, in athletic shorts and a sweat-stained HU tee, hands laced behind his head, arms bulging, as he loped down the hill toward him. His summer-tan skin was rosy with exertion and slick with sweat, and for a handful of seconds, Ezra forgot all about Hudson Selby, too caught up in fantasies about how Noah Becker's sweat-slicked muscle would look in a decidedly more adult context.

Until Noah opened his mouth. "Mr. R.?"

And brought Ezra right back to memories of scraped knees and sandcastles. "Ezra, please."

Noah lowered his arms, and Ezra almost missed what he said next, distracted again by rippling muscles. "You live here?"

He shook off the thoughts he shouldn't be having about his son's childhood best friend. "Just moved in." He pointed at the building behind him, the last in the complex at the bottom of the hill. "Unit R-4."

Noah jutted a thumb toward the front of the complex, near the entrance. "Unit A-2." He ducked his chin and ran a hand over his nape. "Sorry about the whistle. I've just been admiring that car all week whenever I saw it around town. Didn't realize it was yours."

Ezra pretended not to be disappointed that the whistle hadn't been for him.

"She's a beauty." Noah's gaze swept the length of the shiny black AMG GLE coupe before roving back to him, a brow raised. "Midlife-crisis car?"

He gasped in mock outrage. "Past midlife, thank you very much." Chuckling, he shouldered the two bags of groceries, then slammed the trunk closed. "Retirement gift to myself."

"Nice gift." Noah stepped close enough to pat the coupe's spoiler, and Ezra fought against the temptation to inhale. "You'll get your use out of her at the beach, at least until it gets cold. Sadly, winter is a thing here. Not like New York winters but still winter."

"Hopefully I'm out of here before the snow hits."

"End of the semester, right?"

Ezra nodded.

"We might get a few flurries toward year-end, but you should be safe. Worst of it isn't usually until January."

"You've been here long enough to know?"

He shrugged in answer, far short of what Ezra was hoping to learn. "I'll let you get back to it."

"I wanted to tell you thank you," Ezra blurted in quite possibly the most embarrassing verbal vomit ever. Definitely unbecoming of a fifty-eight-year-old. Totally uncharacteristic of a professional dealmaker. But the attraction and guilt that warred in Ezra's chest was knocking him off-balance. He used the excuse of reshouldering the bags to get his words together again. "Thank you for the meals this week at Blue Plate," he said. "Abel was right. Your cooking is something else."

The satisfaction that danced in Noah's eyes before he averted them did nothing to quell Ezra's internal battle. "I'm glad you enjoyed it," he said. Before Ezra could ask what part of culinary school Noah had enjoyed the most, Noah beat him to a different question, jutting his chin toward Ezra's bags. "What's for dinner?"

"Squash casserole." And because Ezra didn't know when to stop, he added, "Couldn't get enough of it."

Noah's answering blush was the last thing Ezra needed and everything he wanted.

Chapter Four

Noah was in the kitchen at Hanover's LGBTQIA+ youth center, putting the final touches on the night's food, when Candice's voice drifted down the hall.

"Noah left a tray of food at the diner. I needed to bring it over." A pause, then her voice grew louder as she approached. "Sounds good. I'll meet you at home in thirty."

Noah chuckled at Candice's bullshit excuse. All his trays were present and accounted for. But were all the kids? He'd bet the spread in front of him that that was the real reason Candice was there. Like him, she was keen to support a safe place for teens and young adults in the same position they'd both been in—on the run because of who they were and who they loved. They'd never talked about his past, but he figured she'd put it together, her invite to start helping out here as much a sign as any. But she didn't pry any further, despite how much she liked to gossip with Holly. He showed her the same courtesy about her past.

"We all good?" Candice asked as she snuck into the kitchen.

He played along rather than call her on her well-intentioned BS. "You tell me?" He gestured at the trays of colorful food. Prosciutto and melon skewers, balsamic watermelon cubes, lamb sliders with tahini slaw, ricotta-stuffed squash blossoms, and fresh mushroom focaccia. Did some of the kids turn up their noses at the fancy food? Sure. But most came around. They were no less deserving of beautiful, delicious food—bright and nutritious, good for the body and soul—than the richest person in town. And Noah appreciated the opportunity to stretch his culinary wings beyond Blue Plate's menu.

"Stunning as always." Candice popped a watermelon cube into her mouth and hummed with delight. She filched another. "Delicious too."

Chuckling, he sprinkled the rest of the cubes with red pepper flakes. "You missed the best part."

And a third disappeared. "You doing okay?"

He was surprised her question was about him and not the kids. "I'm good. Why?"

"You've been quiet this week." How was that any different from usual? "And not your typical gentle giant quiet." She snagged a slice of focaccia. "Holly said something about a run-in with Abel's friend. Ezra, was it?"

Noah averted his gaze. Holly was lovably nosy, but Candice, he didn't doubt, was genuinely concerned. Sure, she let him have his secrets, but she also had his back. That was her way with everyone at Blue Plate, the family she had created, even for temporary members like him. He didn't want to worry her, but now there was someone in Hanover who knew about Hudson Selby, and he didn't know what the fallout from that might be. How it might affect his timeline or Candice's. "Ezra's someone I knew from before."

She laid a hand over his. "Is he safe?"

Of course his safety was the first place her mind jumped. "He's safe." That word meant something different—something more—to them than it did to the average person. He didn't use it lightly. "He—his family—helped me escape. They're the reason I'm here. The reason I'm alive."

She didn't look completely convinced, but when he held a piece of prosciutto-wrapped melon out to her, she let it go. "Okay, but if it ever gets unsafe, you tell me." She looked away and fiddled with rearranging the plates. "Or you go ahead and leave if you need to."

He swallowed around the lump in his throat. "Thank you." Then aiming to cut the tension, he handed her another slice of focaccia. "And I promise to tell you first. A real promise. Unlike that bullshit one you gave Kari on the way in here."

"Whose side are you on?" she said with a sideways glare.

"I plead the Fifth." Their teasing chatter continued as they inspected the trays a final time, then carried them into the main meeting room. Noah had just slid his onto the buffet table when Jordan's laughter from across the room drew his attention. Shelter success stories like Jordan—from malnourished runaway to a business major with farm-to-table dreams—never failed to put a smile on Noah's face. His joy, however, evaporated when Jordan shifted and revealed who he was talking to. The cement floor turned to sand beneath Noah's feet, not the warm powdery kind he liked to dig his toes into but the wet sort that raced out with the tide, defying his balance. "He's here?"

Candice stepped in front of him, redirecting his line of sight. "Ezra's the one speaking tonight. Last-minute cancellation, and Abel roped him in." She covered his wringing hands with her warm ones. "That's why I needed to be sure," she added quietly.

Sure that he was safe; she always had his back. And despite the momentary imbalance, he *was* safe. For the moment. He had made it a whole week with Ezra in town and at Blue Plate with no incidents and no other unexpected visitors. He still needed to go but not right this second. Right this second, he needed to be there for the kids, and at least through the early semester rush, he needed to be at Blue Plate for Candice. He clasped her hands and tugged her close, telling her, "Thank you," once more, his heart warming and feet steadying as he better understood the context and the unwavering support she'd given him.

She returned the hug until they were jostled apart by hungry youths. Their excitement further steadied Noah, putting him on solid ground again by the time Ezra approached. He shared their excitement, his blue eyes alight. "This looks even more amazing than what you serve at Blue Plate."

"He uses this place as his test kitchen," Candice whispered conspiratorially, then held out a hand. "Candice Sims."

"Ezra Rosin," he said, shaking her hand. "Nice to officially meet you." They exchanged small talk about his time in town so far before he returned his attention to Noah. "Kids as taste testers?"

"Who do you think taught me?" The words were out before he considered who might overhear them, but it was impossible not to acknowledge the truth with Ezra standing right in front of him, impossible not to remember how Mr. and Mrs. R. would bring home Michelin-star leftovers for him and Ty and how they'd use their kitchen island to spread out samples of hors d'oeuvres and canapés to taste and approve for whatever party they were hosting next.

Noah understood more about those parties now, recalled Ezra with a full-body flush similar to the one now creeping up his neck. Pink cheeks had no right to look so appealing on a redhead, especially not on his former best friend's father. Noah's own face warmed, embarrassment from a lifetime ago tangling with the first sparks of attraction in the present.

Candice swooped in with the save. "Explain the logic."

"Kids are picky eaters," Noah said. "Their taste buds are still developing, but at their age, they've had fewer chances for someone to badly cook something like brussels sprouts. One bad boiled experience and it's over. Bacon was made to love them."

Ezra laughed. "Kids also tell you when something tastes bad."

Another memory broke through. "Like those sushi rolls."

"Salt cod and beets." Ezra canted at the waist, clutching his stomach, half groaning, half laughing. "I still think the chef must have switched the cod and halibut. It should have been good, but..."

Noah split a grin between Ezra and a bemused Candice. "Single worst bite of food in my life."

Candice stole another watermelon cube. "Hopefully no one feels that way about your food."

"Never!" came a fourth voice as Annie, Candice's sister-in-law and another shelter volunteer, joined them. "Thanks, as always, for the food," she said to him and Candice, then to Ezra, "And thank you, Mr. Rosin, for answering my uncle's call." She shifted the snoozing infant on her hip and held out a hand. "I'm Annie Sims, and this little devil"—she kissed the baby's head—"is Charlie."

"Ezra, please, and it was the least I could do." His gaze strayed again to Noah's, and there was more in those blue depths than Noah could ever hope to unpack.

"I need to make a few announcements, then I'll introduce you." She patted Charlie's back. "Get some food in you. The kids will have a million questions afterward, and the food will go poof." She made a snatching gesture in the air. "You don't want to miss the best part."

"And I better get going," Candice said, "before Kari sends out a search party."

Annie groaned dramatically. "Please save my husband from that call."

Ezra's puzzled expression pried Noah's laughter free.

"Kari's brother, Annie's husband, is a cop. There was a little too much excitement last year."

"But it had a happy ending." Annie threw a wink over her shoulder as she headed for the front. "Ask Abel sometime."

"Or you can fill me in?" Ezra said to Noah.

A surprised, "Sure," popped out before Noah could catch it. He'd been avoiding Ezra all week, so why was he serving up an excuse for further conversation? He backtracked in a hurry. "I need to walk Candice out."

She shooed off the suggestion and rose on her toes, pecking his cheek. "I'll be fine and so will you."

He waited for her to leave, then asked Ezra, who was nibbling from the colorful collection on his plate, "Got a favorite?"

"The squash blossoms."

"I remember how the bodegas would only get them for two weeks in late summer, and Ty and I would visit them all." His insides warmed at the mental picture of him and his best friend scouring the Upper East Side markets, filling their totes with the fragile yellow flowers. "We'd get as many as we could."

Ezra's smile was as fond as Noah's memory. "And then we'd have to eat them all that weekend because they wilt so fast." His smile turned wistful, then faded. "I didn't know you'd be here tonight." He lowered his chin and ran a hand over his nape. "I know I've been at Blue Plate a lot this week. The food's just so damn good. I didn't mean to crowd you here too."

Squash blossoms unfurled in Noah's chest. "You didn't

and thank you." He wanted to keep talking to Ezra, at least in that moment. "We do the food for special events here. I need to give back."

Ezra's face whipped up. "I thought Abel said this place was new?"

"This particular shelter, yeah. But I landed in a place like this after that night."

"How long have you been in Hanover?"

"A few years."

Ezra's forehead wrinkled, no doubt trying to account for the missing decade. A period Noah didn't want to remember in detail; years filled with close calls that had sent him scurrying and more downs than ups. He shook his head and stepped away from the past. And from Ezra, the distance between them having narrowed. "I need to get the rest out of the kitchen," he said, "so I can top off the trays."

He started that direction but Ezra's, "Hey, Noah," made him pause. Ezra's hand froze in midair like he'd intended to reach for Noah but stopped himself. He drew it back and raked his fingers through his copper mane. Stunning. And mind-blowing how Mr. R. looked better in his late fifties than he had in his midforties.

"I was wondering if I could cook for you sometime."

Noah rocked on his heels, the waves rushing back in, wet sand giving way. "Ezra—"

"As a thank-you and a chance for you to tell me that long story. I need to get up to speed on all the town gossip." His gaze bounced to the squash blossoms, then back to Noah. "I bought some squash blossoms this morning. Can't eat them all myself."

Another excuse fell from Noah's lips. "They won't last past tomorrow."

Ezra snatched it up. "So dinner tomorrow, then?"

Everything about the offer, about Ezra's presence, felt safe. As it always had. "All right."

Everything except the rosy blush that returned to Ezra's cheeks, that had the squash blossoms in Noah's chest reaching for the sun.

Chapter Five

Ezra's phone vibrated where it sat on the dining table, and thinking it might be Noah, he scurried out from the kitchen to peek at the screen.

Archer Scott.

Not Noah but also not a call he could ignore. He wiped both hands on his apron and slid a mostly clean finger across the screen to answer. "Two seconds, Archer." He snatched his earbuds off their charger in the living room and popped them in. "You there?"

"I'm here."

"How's harvest looking?" Ezra adjusted the volume on his way back to the kitchen. "Not that it's technically any of my business yet."

The chuckle on the other end of the line was warm and gruff, two descriptors that were not mutually exclusive when describing his friend. "It's good, Ezra, and it *is* your business. You own this dirt now, even if the business and legal possession don't transfer to you until January. How the vines do year over year matters for your short- and long-term prospects. It's good for me to see."

"How did I get lucky enough to find you?"

"I fucked your wife."

"And me." Ezra sliced a lime and spritzed it over the pineapple and golden beet salsa. "Or did you forget who approached who first?"

"Did I forget the sexy ginger who sauntered across the room in red lace briefs and told me his wife wanted to boss me around for the evening? Of course not."

Ezra was sure the grin on the other end of the line was crooked, the same devilish smirk that had caught Ezra's attention at a party in Santa Barbara years ago. Ezra and Al had ended up spending the entire weekend with Archer and had occasionally played together since. A friendship— a foundation of trust—that made trusting his winery's grapes to Archer, an experienced winemaker, a no-brainer.

"Sparkling is in the tanks," Archer said. "All the vermentino and arneis are picked. The brix on the aglianico are about a week out. The barbera and sangi should be a couple weeks after that."

Ezra put a lid on the bowl of salsa, shook it gently, then stuck it in the fridge to marinate. "Bit late this year?"

"No, this is actually on schedule. Mother Nature decided not to shit her pantsuit for a change. No major floods this spring, no major fires this summer, no outrageous heat waves or cold snaps. No trauma to the vines or grapes. We're right on time."

Ezra eyed the bottle of arneis chilling on the top shelf of the fridge. The same vintage as the bottle that had convinced him to make either the smartest or dumbest business decision of his life.

Outcome to be determined.

Same as that evening's uncertain outcome—as to the food and the company. Quesadillas and fish tacos were personal favorites, but did Noah like them? Would he tell Ezra if he didn't? Ezra wanted to learn all those details about him, to get to know the man he'd become. But Ezra would be lying if he said he wasn't also attracted to said man. From his haunting gray eyes to that beard that would tickle and scratch in all the right places, to the extra inches and heft that could pin Ezra down while Noah ordered...

Ezra closed his eyes and pumped the brakes on the spiraling fantasy. If Noah had been anyone other than Tyler's childhood best friend, Ezra would've made him a dozen indecent proposals by now.

"Ezra, you there?" Archer said, drawing his attention back to their conversation.

"Yeah, sorry, just in the middle of cooking." A reasonable enough excuse. "You were saying?"

"I was saying it's a good crop. You've got interesting, challenging varietals that will appeal to casual drinkers and wine enthusiasts. I've already been talking to some of the soms and collectors up here. The demand is there."

Archer's assurance and the excitement in his voice eased some of Ezra's anxiety, about the winery at least. "You sound like a kid in a candy store."

"When you offered me an insane amount of money to leave Lompoc and come up here, I'd resigned myself to chard and pinot. No more Wild Wild West of varietals like they were cultivating in the Santa Rita Hills. Then you showed me the list of vine stock, and I about shit my pantsuit. I get to keep playing winemaker cowboy."

Ezra laughed. "And you're sure you didn't mind the move? Or working for me, given our history?" It had been a lot to ask—to uproot his life, sell his home, and break his employment contract with a more established winery—all for a shot on him and acres of temperamental Italian grapes on a misty hillside in Sonoma County.

"I like a challenge," Archer said. "New weather patterns, new soils, new people. A culture where wine is front and center. And I made a mint on the house. So no, I didn't mind the move. And things were getting uncomfortable in Lompoc with the shifting mood in the military."

Ezra lowered the block of queso fresco he'd been crumbling. "You didn't tell me you were feeling unsafe."

"I'm kinky and queer. None of us are ever completely safe. But it feels a whole hell of a lot safer here in the Bay Area and working for you."

Relief washed over the flare of concern. "Good. I'm glad I could make that happen."

"And nothing's going to happen with us. I can't give you what you need."

And he wouldn't be able to give Archer what he needed either, sexually or in the relationship department. He was the furthest thing from marriage material these days, and Archer was on the hunt, another reason the Bay

Area had appealed to him. Ezra was just lucky to get him as a professional partner. "I trust you," he said.

"Exactly."

"Is Al around?"

"Probably, if she's dressed yet."

Ezra rolled his eyes as he shredded mozzarella into the bowl with the other cheese. "I thought you were there to run my winery through its paces, not my ex-wife."

"What can I say, she beckoned, I followed orders. Mmm, what that woman can make me do with a wheel and some pulleys..."

"Is that necessary?" came the husky voice of the woman herself. A muffled handoff later, Al spoke directly to Ezra. "Hey, you."

"I'm paying him to work."

"Oh, I made him work."

Ezra couldn't help but laugh. "I love you."

"I know, I love you too." Her smirk was no doubt as devilish as Archer's. "How's it going there?"

It was on the tip of his tongue to mention Noah, to talk through his conflict with the person he trusted most in the world, but Noah had asked him not to tell Al and Tyler he was in Hanover. Noah had trusted him with his secret and his safety. Hadn't Ezra just been concerned about Archer's? Granted, Noah seemed safe in Hanover, and Ezra was sure Al wouldn't tell a soul, not even Tyler, if Ezra told her secrecy was important. But if Ezra wanted to get to know Noah again, if he wanted to see where that forbidden spark of attraction might lead, he couldn't betray Noah's trust to anyone, not even Al.

"Ezra, you feeling okay?"

"I'm fine, and things are going well here." He traded the box grater for a chef's knife and began slicing scallions. "The students want to learn, and I'm learning to slow down and explain things."

"Good. What about slowing down in general? That was half the point of this. Been out on the boat with Abel yet?"

"This morning actually. Still can't fish. Didn't catch a damn thing. Luckily, Abel shared, otherwise no fish tacos. I'd be serving only squash blossom quesadillas for dinner."

"Those sound delicious with or without the fish tacos. You serving Abel and Rachel?"

"No, um..." He flailed, which gave Al too much fodder, so he went with as much truth as he could give without breaking Noah's confidence. "One of the neighbors."

"A hot neighbor?"

Well, yes, but he wasn't going to give her *that* much. "Why don't you go back to fucking Archer?"

"Should have time before I have to drive back to San Francisco." He was sure she'd manage to squeeze that in somehow. "Oh, by the way, Ty said something about bringing the family out there soon. Maybe when he's in Raleigh wooing some chef he's got his eye on."

Apprehension rose on a wave of panic. Chances were good Ty would run into Noah if he visited. But unlike the earlier unease Ezra hadn't known what to do with, the high-anxiety spike of adrenaline was familiar. He was a deal junkie. He knew how to work a problem to get the result he wanted. "I'll call him and sort it. Molly would probably have more fun in Wilmington or Raleigh anyway."

"And Sloan will have more fun anywhere there are extra hands."

He cringed in sympathy as he gently handled the squash blossoms, making sure they were dry. "Michael still teething?"

"Yeah, that's why I need to get back. But I wanted to go over the plans and permit applications with Archer in person."

They intended to make the winery biodynamic, but that required improvements in the fields and to the facility, as did the restaurant he and Ty wanted to open on-site. "You think everything will get approved?"

Al had been practicing real estate law for thirty years, including land use and planning, and she'd teamed with local counsel in their daughter-in-law's firm. "We should be good for the hearing. The improvements are in everyone's interest. I'll get the permits. Don't you worry."

"Thank you. I couldn't be here if it weren't for you, Tyler, Sloan, and Archer." He was asking a lot of them, managing aspects of his new venture while he was effectively on sabbatical, doctor ordered, but he felt like he wasn't carrying his share of the load. Like maybe this wasn't the best venture at all if he might not be there for the long-term. A legacy, he'd convinced himself, but had he put himself ahead of others again?

Al quickly disabused him of the notion. "And stop feeling guilty. About all of it. I don't care where you are on this Earth as long as you're on it, alive and kicking, so you stay right there where you need to be, fishing and having dinner with your hot neighbor. We'll handle this until you get here, then we'll enjoy it as a family."

Before he could get a "thank you" or "I love you" past the lump in his throat, Archer shouted, "Al, you want in on this?"

Words erupted on a watery chuckle. "Do I want to know?"

"About my feet all over your precious grapes? Probably not. Love you."

"Love you too."

He hung up, chest filled with warmth, a smile stretched across his face. Things were coming together there at the winery, his future falling into place. His smile dimmed. Was it fair to start something with Noah in the present in Hanover? He'd have to be clear anything to come of it would only be short-term. And why the fuck was he jumping fourteen steps ahead of dinner with an old family friend?

He yanked the bottle of arneis out of the fridge, screwed off the top, and poured himself a generous glass. He took a long slow sip and savored the crisp yet mellow flavors. Refreshing. He'd made the right call, buying the land and vines that produced the grapes for the beautiful wine. And he'd made the right call about tonight too. It was just dinner, a chance to get reacquainted. There was no way he'd ever get past the vision in his head of Hudson and Tyler building sandcastles on the shore.

A knock sounded against the door. Ezra finished his wine, then went to greet his dinner guest. He swung open the door and a tide of desire flattened the sandcastles. Dressed in low-slung jeans and a snug tee with his hair pulled back and an apron in hand, Noah was everything Ezra wanted.

And when he grinned, an easy, "Put me to work, chef," falling from his lips, want edged dangerously toward need.

Chapter Six

Noah was tempted to lick the remains of spiced crema from his fingers, but he did the polite thing instead and used his napkin. "You can still cook."

Across the table, Ezra lounged in his chair and sipped his wine. "You sound surprised."

"I forgot how well."

"I'll take that as a compliment."

"Was meant to be one." The fish tacos with the crema and a tangy citrus slaw were fresh yet savory, the beet salsa earthy yet tropical, and the squash blossom quesadillas were crunchy on the outside and sweet and gooey on the inside. Perfect contrasts, each dish, all complemented by the crisp white wine. "Really, Ezra, everything was great, but this wine"—he tipped his glass to the chef—"and those quesadillas were standouts."

Ezra smiled, the picture of relaxed, confident, and effortlessly sexy in jeans and a dark tee with Chess stitched on the pocket. Like Damian Lewis in one of those *Billions* episodes where he strutted around in bespoke jeans and a Metallica tee while making, well, billions. It was all Noah could do to focus on Ezra's words and not on how his plump lower lip contrasted perfectly with his thin upper one.

"Quesadillas are one of my favorites. Versatile, given all the ways you can fill them, and relatively easy to make." He finished his wine, then twirled the empty glass by the stem. "And I'm glad you enjoyed the wine. It's the vintage that convinced me to buy the place."

"The winery?" At Ezra's nod, Noah rotated the bottle to read the label. "You gonna keep the name?" He tried and failed not to butcher the Italian he couldn't translate. "La Montagna Nebbiosa."

"I think I have to. It means misty mountain."

Noah laughed out loud as a once favorite tune drifted through his head. "You played that Zeppelin record all the time."

"Whenever I was rereading *Lord of the Rings*," he said with a wink. "Al bought me a bottle as a gag gift when I—" He cut himself off and rubbed a hand over his chest.

When he what? Noah wanted the answer, wanted the words Ezra had held back, but he didn't want to pry. He also wanted to know why Ezra and Mrs. R. had divorced. He spoke so fondly of her still—his best friend he'd called her—so what had driven them apart?

Ezra saved him from derailing a perfectly nice evening with awkward questions. "Lucky surprise the wine was good," he said. "And lucky the owners were looking to sell."

Noah savored the last swallow from his glass. "Thank you for sharing."

Ezra straightened from his slouch and began stacking plates. "Thank *you* for sharing all the Hanover gossip." Rather than stare at the slice of freckled skin exposed by Ezra's hiked shirt hem, Noah helped collect and carry dishes to the sink. "Those Shakespeare murders last year sound wild." He filled the sink with soap and water. "I'm sorry it ended with Abel leaving the department, but I'm happy for his nieces. Sounds like they got their happily ever afters."

"Abel too with Rachel and with more time to fish."

"He's damn good at it. Caught that mahi I used for the fish tacos." Ezra opened the fridge and pointed to the filets on ice in the coldest part of the fridge. "And those are for tomorrow."

Noah recognized the white and pink flesh and shimmery silver skin. "Spanish mackerel. Lucky you."

"Gonna pan sear it up with some sweet peppers and thyme."

"I *think* I trust you to treat it right."

"Hey now!" Ezra hip-checked him on the way to grabbing a towel. "You were just waxing poetic about my cooking."

"I don't wax poetic."

"Semantics." Ezra rolled his eyes and flicked the top of the sudsy water. Bubbles flew into the air, dancing and popping between them. "Maybe you should join me so you can be sure tonight's meal wasn't a fluke?"

Noah ducked his chin, pretending to focus on the

dishes, not on the fizzy feelings in his chest. Bubbles dancing through his blood, threatening to pop into more poetic words on his tongue. Like how much he enjoyed the playful banter, how much he needed these reminders of the good parts of his old life, how much he wanted to say *yes* to dinner again tomorrow. He shouldn't, though. He couldn't risk dinners with Ezra becoming a regular thing that might put him in danger, no matter how much Noah enjoyed his company.

"No pressure, Noah." Ezra lightly touched his shoulder, then put several steps between them. "I just like making and sharing food."

The distance so effortlessly given, the care and consideration Ezra always exercised around him, made Noah want to scoot closer again. Made him feel safe. Like when he'd hung out at the Rosins' growing up. Like he tried to make folks feel at Blue Plate and the shelter. "It's something, isn't it? To see food you've poured your heart and soul into make someone else's heart and soul happy."

He handed a dripping plate to Ezra, who graced him with an earnest smile. The kind and sexy combo was devastating, his words even more so. "You deserve to be happy, Noah."

Comfortable, familiar warmth filled the space between them as they washed dishes, Noah scrubbing and Ezra drying and putting them away. Space that was tighter in Ezra's kitchen than in the one in Noah's unit. Every brushed elbow, every light touch against his back when Ezra stepped behind him sent heat rippling beneath Noah's skin. He kept his face angled down, acting as if washing dishes was the most interesting thing in the world, hoping Ezra didn't notice the blush creeping up his neck. No telling if there was one on Ezra's sunburned face. Noah doubted it. The Rosins had always been comfortable in their own skin, safe in their own space, filling it with laughter, affection, and gentle, easy touches.

"You're comfortable here? In Hanover?" Ezra said as if reading his mind.

Noah nodded. "Random serial killer aside, Hanover's a good town with good people and good work. Between the tourists and the university, we're always busy at the diner. There's not an off-season, but that doesn't mean it's nonstop like New York."

"Not at all." Ezra rolled his shoulders back. "I've only been here a week, and muscles I didn't know I had are unknotting."

"Or it's just the sunburn melting them away."

Ezra chuckled. "I underestimated how long we'd be out there."

Noah peeked at Ezra from under his lashes. He was wrong before. He *could* see Ezra's blush beneath the sunburn. "The glow looks good on you." Ezra's breath caught, and his gaze shot up, clashing with Noah's. Pupils dilated, they invited Noah to fall into them, into Ezra. Noah slammed on the brakes before he made the dive. "You also look like a lobster."

Ezra laughed, uneven at first but then more fully. "More sunscreen next time." He covered his fist with the towel, then gently dried the inside of the first wine glass. "I'm not surprised you stay busy. I'm sure the elevated diner food you serve at Blue Plate keeps the people streaming in."

"I like comfort food. It's what I needed and what I can give back." Noah finished rinsing the second glass. "But nothing says comfort food can't also be artistic and challenging for me and my diners."

"I bet you loved culinary school."

"Didn't go."

Ezra gasped, his hand flexed, and he bobbled the wine glass. Noah tried to steady it, their fingers brushing, tangling as more bubbles fizzed and popped, inside and out. The glass fell through their fingertips, hitting the floor and shattering into pieces.

Waking Noah's kitchen instincts. "Step back," he ordered.

Ezra immediately obeyed, stepping out of the circle of glass and back against the kitchen island. Chin lowered, his breathing was heavy and his knuckles were white where they gripped the edge of the island. Was he freaking out? Noah's voice had been sharp, the "yes, chef" one Jordan often teased him about. Breaking glass was a professional trigger, a trained one that propelled him to act fast and protect his team. But had he inadvertently tripped one of Ezra's personal triggers? Between therapy and the shelter, Noah understood that everyone had them, big and small.

Or did Ezra think he'd upset Noah by dropping the glass? Had Noah's bark sounded dangerous? Like Noah's father's? Surely, Ezra didn't think... *Fuck!*

He tossed his towel over the biggest pieces of glass,

stepped around the rest, and moved in front of Ezra. "It's okay," he spoke softly. "It was just a—"

Ezra lifted his chin, and it was Noah's turn to gasp. He was triggered all right, but not in a bad way. His pupils were blown wide, only a thin ring of blue left around them, and the blush coloring Ezra's cheeks was unmistakable, even under the sunburn.

Noah remembered that look. If it hadn't been the worst night of his life the first time he'd seen it, twenty-year-old Noah would have been hard as a rock. Thirty-three-year-old Noah was sure getting there fast.

Ezra swiped his tongue across his bottom lip, wetting it on a shaky breath, his eyes never leaving Noah's. Fire licked at Noah's heels, propelling him closer, even though he knew he should run the opposite direction. He pitched his voice low—commanding—again. "Hand me a towel." Ezra immediately complied, snatching a towel from behind him, sight unseen, and shoving it into Noah's hand.

Noah's dick ached, and he cursed, high and breathy himself.

The shift in his tone seemed to snap Ezra out of whatever space he'd slipped into, the other man's eyes fluttering closed as he inhaled a deep shuddery breath. "Shit." He shifted left, out from between Noah and the island, then crouched to retrieve a hand broom and dustpan from a lower cabinet. "I'm sorry."

Noah adjusted himself and knelt beside him, carefully removing the towel so Ezra could sweep up the glass. "You don't need to apologize. I shouldn't have—"

"You don't need to apologize either." Ezra stood and tossed the shards into the garbage. "For anything."

They fumbled around each other, neither meeting the other's eyes, each careful not to brush arms, elbows, or hands. It was a very different kind of moment from the charged one they'd just shared. Despite Ezra's words, Noah regretted what he'd done, regretted thinking with his dick and not his head, regretted the awkwardness that had rushed into the comfortable space between them as a result.

Ezra's space, which he'd invaded and made uncomfortable.

"I'm gonna go," Noah said.

"Probably for the best."

Stomach sinking further, Noah had to force himself to walk, not run, to the door. He paused over the threshold. It had been a wonderful evening before he'd gone and fucked it up. "Thank you for dinner. For sharing with me."

Ezra finally met his gaze again. A stormy mix of emotions, too many for Noah to sort, swirled in his bright blue eyes, but his smile seemed genuine. As did his words. "Thank you for letting me."

Noah held on to that smile, those words, as he made the short walk back to his apartment, hoping like hell he hadn't just severed the connection to the good parts of his past he was beginning to realize he desperately missed.

Chapter Seven

Noah tossed his tasting spoon into the sink, stainless steel clanking against stainless steel, and raised his voice to be heard over the racket. "This isn't right." He gestured at the pot of simmering soup. "The flavors are off, I can smell the croutons burning, and the number of carrots you wasted—"

"Shit!" Jordan spun, grabbed a mitt, and snatched the tray of charred croutons out of the oven. "I'm sorry, boss."

"There's another whole crate of carrots in the storeroom," Alicia said as she stepped to Jordan's side. "We're not gonna run out."

"Yeah, boss man, chill," Holly chimed in. She leaned a hip against the end of the prep table near them and folded her arms. "You've been snappy going on two weeks now. I can't carry the orders out any faster than you sling 'em, Jordan can't read your mind, and Alicia shouldn't have to keep apologizing for your bad mood."

Alicia's and Holly's words sank in, as did Jordan's terrified expression, and Noah mentally face-palmed, then did it for real. "Fuck, I'm sorry." He wiped a hand down his face, then spread his arms. "Bring it in?" His team embraced with a collective sigh of relief, which drew one out of Noah too. "This is on me, not you. I'm sorry."

"Guy issues?" Holly asked. "Professor Sexy?"

He rolled his eyes, then recalled how Ezra had done the same during the dinner they'd shared. Going on two weeks ago. The last time he'd seen Ezra. Aromas of carrot and ginger hit his nose, and more realizations dawned. Carrot-ginger soup was one of Ezra's favorites. As was yesterday's squash casserole. As were most of the blue plate specials he'd prepared the past two weeks. All for naught.

"Mmhmm," Holly drew out. "I know that look. Man trouble." Explanation enough for her, today at least, thanks to the packed diner she had to get back to. She spun on her heel and exited through the swinging door.

"You good?" Alicia asked.

"All good."

Satisfied, she followed Holly out to the dining room, leaving only him and Jordan in the kitchen. The younger cook slipped out from under his arm and dipped a fresh tasting spoon into the soup. He sipped it, then shook his head. "You're right, boss. Something's off."

"And I should have explained *what* instead of snapping. I'm sorry," he said again, then spent the next half hour working with Jordan on the soup between other orders. Explaining the carrot to ginger balance, how to punch up the stock with a dash of curry, how to add acidity with a sprinkle of sumac, how to round the carrots in order to make the most of the product and cook it evenly.

"You got this?" Noah asked, once Jordan was hard at work preparing carrots for a new batch.

"I've got it," Jordan said without looking up. "Thank you."

"You're welcome." He finished plating an order, sent the ready ring to Holly, then slipped out the door to the parking lot. He leaned back against the brick wall, head tilted to the sky, and breathed deep.

He hated getting tense with his team. He'd worked hard not to be the kind of boss, the kind of person, who snapped and shouted. He wouldn't be like his father, not if he could help it. He wanted everyone at Blue Plate to enjoy coming to work, to feel safe there. Like he did. He hadn't meant to let the blip in his personal life bleed into his professional one. He hadn't meant to let Ezra be a blip at all, but he couldn't get the mental picture of a turned-on Ezra out of his head. And even though he shouldn't want to see it again—Ezra was Tyler's father for fuck's sake—he did. Hell, he just wanted to see Ezra again, period. But had he gone too far? Pushed Ezra too far? Or had Ezra realized being around him was too big a risk for himself and for his family? Was Noah too unsafe to be around for multiple reasons?

Speaking of unsafe... the squeal of tires made Noah open his eyes, then run as he recognized Candice's Tahoe screaming into the parking lot. She'd barely thrown open the car door when Noah was there, grasping the frame, a knot of worry in his chest. "What's wrong?"

"You're asking me?" She took his offered hand and slid out of the seat, her feet touching the running rail, then the ground. She slammed the car door shut behind her. "Holly called and said to get down here. That you were on the warpath."

"Did she actually say that?"

"No, what she actually said was, 'He's not getting dick from Professor Sexy, and he's a blue-ball monster,' but I edited."

Noah laughed, the first time in days—eleven to be exact. He slumped next to Candice against the SUV. "You didn't need to edit. I needed the laugh. And you didn't need to rush over here."

She cocked a brow like she didn't believe him. Smart lady. "What happened with Ezra?"

"You know, Professor Sexy could mean someone else?"

"I'd agree if Trevor Caldwell was still at HU, but he's not, so spill."

He pushed off the side of the car, out of its shadow and into the sun. It was one of the things he loved about Hanover. Few buildings here were tall enough to blot out the sun; not like in New York. The sun's warmth was everywhere. Made difficult things easier to talk about. "I had dinner at his place a couple weeks back. Haven't seen him since."

"You gotta give me more than that."

He dug a toe into the gravel. "It was good, easy, like settling back in with an old friend."

"That night at the shelter, I got the impression y'all went *way* back."

"I was best friends with his son, Tyler. We lived in the same building, across the hall from the Rosins."

"You said they helped you escape. From your dad?"

He nodded. "He was abusive. Tyler found out a few months before I left. I lied and told him it was the first time, that I had a plan to get out. Anything so he wouldn't tell his parents. I knew if he told them, they'd get involved. They're good people. But then Dad found out I was gay and almost killed me."

"Jesus, Noah." Carefully, in his line of sight, she reached out and laid a gentle hand on his forearm. "I'm sorry."

He covered her hand with his. "I imagine you have a similar story."

"I do, and I know it's a minefield you still tiptoe through every day. I won't push. You tell me what you need to, and you *do* what you need to."

He squeezed her hand, then released it and a little more of his truth. "Things deteriorated after that two years earlier than I'd planned. Ty got me out of there and to his parents' place in the Hamptons. They took care of me." He rubbed a hand over his nape, brushing away the lingering phantom pain, and flexed his ankle that still ached each spring, no matter how much strength training he did. "They gave me what I needed to get away from him."

"And now you're worried your dad will use them to find you?"

"I don't care about *me*. I don't want him to retaliate against *them* for helping me and because he's a homophobic asshole."

"Ezra's queer too, yeah? I mean, Holly said so, then I saw the way he was checking you out at the shelter."

"He was not, and oh yeah, he most definitely is." He'd witnessed that much, but also Ezra had told the shelter kids he was pansexual during his talk.

"He most definitely was, and now you're a blue-ball monster because he ghosted you after dinner together. Tell me about it. If you need to talk it out."

He smiled, and he suspected it was fond like Ezra's had been. "He was Mr. R. to start, but the more we talked —about food, his winery, Hanover—the more it felt like he was just Ezra, a friend."

"A very handsome friend."

He shot her a sideways grin. "You're as bad as Holly."

She looped an arm around his waist, and he looped one over her shoulders. "We all just want to see you happy. You deserve that."

"Ezra said the same thing."

"What else did Ezra say?"

"It wasn't so much what he said as what happened."

She opened her mouth, tempted to ask for more details, but stopped herself, and he had to laugh, chuckling as he started them toward the diner. "Details aren't really mine to give." Yes, Ezra was out as queer, but Noah didn't know how out he was about his kinks, in which case they were not Noah's to disclose if that's even what he'd witnessed. "Let's just say I may have overstepped, and I haven't seen or heard from him since."

"Maybe he's been busy? Or went back to New York?"

He shook his head. "I see his car come and go from the

apartment complex. I fucked things up." They stopped outside the kitchen door, and Noah lowered his arm. "I just got him back."

She sighed, and after three years in each other's space more days than not, he knew that sound, knew those hands on her hips and the determined set of her jaw.

"Don't give me that look," he said.

"Don't *you* twiddle your thumbs and do nothing. If you don't want to lose him again, stop waiting for him to come to you. Go to him."

There was nothing he wanted to do more, but... "What if he doesn't want to see me?"

She dropped the stern friend act and drew up the caring one instead, a gentle hand on his arm again, a soft encouraging smile for him. "I don't think he would purposefully avoid you after just finding you again either."

Unless Ezra didn't like what he'd found.

Chapter Eight

Ezra looked up from his piles of half-graded essays, the knocking on his door finally penetrating the fog of concentration. How long had that been going on? A while, judging by the escalating volume. Probably another hospitable neighbor, which he appreciated, truly, but he'd made a promise to his students, and he had to get this done. Maybe if he just ignored—

The knocking resumed. "Ezra, are you in there?"

A voice he hadn't heard in ten—eleven?—days other than in his dreams. A voice he'd gotten used to again, its tone deeper and more confident than it had been a decade ago but still with a comforting hint of home.

"Your car's outside," Noah said. "I'm getting worried."

"I'm coming." He tossed his pen onto the coffee table and pushed up from the couch, wincing as joints cracked and muscles protested. What time was it? Or more accurately, what day was it?

He swung through the kitchen, pitched the teetering

stack of days-old takeout containers, and checked his shirt and shorts for embarrassing food stains. Only wrinkles, and there was no help for those. He raked a hand through his hair, no help for that mess either, then peeked out the peephole. And caught his breath. Noah's skin was a deeper tan like he'd spent time in the sun, his snug tee and cargo shorts hugged every defined muscle, and his hair was loose of its tie, the long brown strands of his mohawk falling over the shaved sides. Fuck, how was it possible he was even more handsome than when Ezra had last seen him? Or maybe Ezra had just missed seeing him as much as he'd missed his voice?

Noah lifted an insulated tote in view of the peephole. "Peace offering."

Ezra closed his tired eyes and thunked his forehead against the door. "You don't need to make a peace offering."

"Seems maybe I do."

Stepping back, he opened the door and leaned against the frame. "I'm the one that should make a peace offering. I didn't mean to ghost you."

Noah's gaze raked over him, the worried divot between his brows getting deeper as his gray eyes tracked down and up. Ezra could imagine what he was seeing—bags under his eyes, hair a wavy mess, a way past five o'clock shadow of red and blond stubble. "You do look a bit like Casper. Sunburn's all gone."

"Because I've basically lived here or in Paxton Hall the past two weeks."

"Maybe some comfort food will make you less ghostly."

Ezra sighed, removed his bifocals, and pinched the bridge of his nose.

"Or I can just leave this for you."

The dejection in his voice made Ezra snap his eyes open, made him step back from the edge of exhaustion. He clasped Noah's shoulder, stopping him from setting the bag at his feet. "No, please, come in. I need to take a break." He shifted and opened the door wider. "That sigh wasn't about you. It was me mentally adding vitamin D to the list of supplements I've been forgetting to take."

Noah stepped inside and whistled low. "You ever think about going paperless?"

"Too old for that shit." Though observing things from this perspective, it wasn't a bad idea. He closed the door and scooted around Noah. "Apologies for the mess. This is the problem without Al around to keep me from going full-blown workaholic." He headed for the dining table, but then, not wanting to battle the blueprint rolls for the umpteenth time that day, he diverted to the living room. "Let's go in here." He gathered the stacks of papers off the coffee table, keeping the graded ones separate from the to-be-read ones, and set them on the media stand, his red pen perched on the latter stack to remind him.

"You need that big Camelot table you and Mrs. R. had in New York."

Ezra smiled, remembering all the Halloweens Tyler and Hud—Noah—had dressed up as Knights of the Round Table. The fond memories were a big reason he'd kept the table. He looked forward to making new ones with the next generation of Rosins around it. "It's already on its way to the winery."

Noah straightened from where he was unloading deli containers onto the coffee table. "You still have it?"

He nodded. "Can't kill it, and Al's doing the hoteling thing for work, bouncing between her firm offices. She just rents a furnished place in whatever city she's in that month."

"She's good?"

"Oh yeah. Busy with work and busy fucking my winemaker."

Noah bobbled the breadbasket and cursed as a runaway biscuit rolled Ezra's direction.

He snatched it off the ground and dropped it back in the basket. "Five-second rule," he said with a grin. "As for Archer, he's a mutual friend Al and I played with from time to time." Noah blushed and averted his gaze, biting one corner of his lower lip like he wanted to ask something but wasn't sure how. Ezra gave him something easier to talk about. For now. "What all did you cook? It smells delicious."

Noah cleared his throat and finished unloading the bag. "Carrot-ginger soup, root vegetable pot pies, biscuits, and honey cake, and a favorite brew."

"Oh, my favorite soup."

"I remember."

It was Ezra's turn to avert his gaze, Noah's deep voice and shy smile almost as tempting as the soup. Almost. "Let me get some bowls and things."

"Can I ask what brought on the work hurricane?"

"Perfect-storm scenario." He stacked plates and bowls, added silverware, and tucked a roll of paper towels under his arm. "It's my first time grading papers, and the essays are so good I just get sucked into them. I want to give all the students feedback. Plus, we've got ongoing issues at the winery."

"With the vintage?"

"No, thank God. Archer's ecstatic with the grapes." He gestured at the blueprints on his way back to the kitchen to grab pint glasses. "It's the permits and approvals for renovations that are giving us trouble."

"Are you going to have to go out there?" Noah took the glasses from him and poured the beer while Ezra finished arranging plates before claiming the cushion next to him on the sofa.

"Hopefully not. Al's handling the legal, and Ty and Sloan's best friend, Miller, have connections up there."

"Wait?" Noah froze midpour. "Miller Sykes?"

"The very same." Chuckling, Ezra darted out a hand and tipped the bottle up, saving the beer from overflowing the glass at the last second. "Careful there."

"Shit, sorry!" Noah shook his head as if dislodging the shock and set the bottle and glass on the table. Shifting, he brought one leg up, bent and resting on the cushion near Ezra's thigh. "Your daughter-in-law is Sloan *Thatcher*? The same one who was married to Miller Sykes?"

Noah's eyes were so comically wide Ezra wished he had a camera. Surprise totally transformed Noah's face and gave new meaning to the saying many shades of gray, all of them swirling in his eyes. "So you do follow foodie news?" Ezra teased.

"Hard to miss that bit with everything that went on with his restaurant in Napa, the cancer and remission, and now Chess blowing up like crazy." He slapped a palm to his forehead. "Your T-shirt the other night."

"It's amazing there, the space and what Miller has done with the concept. You'd love it. Similar elevated comfort food vibe." He reached for his bowl of soup, tasted a spoonful, and closed his eyes, savoring. "This is so good."

Noah shifted beside him, and when Ezra opened his eyes again, the chef had crossed his legs and was leaning forward to grab his own bowl. "It's kicked up a bit from the way you used to make it. I'm addicted to curry."

"It's amazing."

"Try it with the beer." Noah jutted his chin toward the bottle. "It's one of my favorite harvest ales. Tastes like fall."

He was right; the beer was perfect with the meal and for relaxing them both. Conversation flowed as they ate and drank, talk about other autumn beers; about the mushrooms, root vegetables, and seasonings Noah had thrown into the veggie pot pies; about the special Rosh Hashanah feast he was planning for the youth center; about Ty and Sloan and their kids; and about the Rosin Hospitality Group that included Ty's restaurants and now the winery.

Talking with Noah was easy, eating his delicious food was even easier, and before Ezra knew it, he'd finished his soup and pot pie and was noshing on his second—third—slice of honey cake. "Thank you for this," he told Noah.

"And truly, I'm sorry about disappearing on you. This"—he gestured around the room at the remnants of the aptly described work hurricane—"was the very habit, the lifestyle, I'm supposed to be taking a break from."

"Hard to take your foot off the gas?"

He laughed. "See past-midlife-crisis car outside." He popped the last bite of cake into his mouth, swallowed, and washed it down with another sip of beer. "My brakes are rusty."

That rust had been part of the reason he and Al had started to crumble. Too many dates and parties missed. Too many connections missed, which had led to him missing when their needs had diverged. Life was supposed to get easier once Ty had left the nest, and it had for a while, but then he'd spiraled inside his glass tower, not that Al wasn't also a workaholic, but she'd always been better at carving out space for their needs. He'd failed her there.

A biscuit appeared in front of his face. "Cathead for your thoughts?"

"All yours. I'm full." He patted his stomach. "I was just thinking about Al."

"You miss her?" Noah asked as he cut open the biscuit and slathered it with the rich black cherry jam he'd made.

"I miss the companionship, the sharing a life part, but I wasn't a very good partner in the end."

"I find that hard to believe."

He gestured again at the papers strewn over half the room. "I pulled a spiral like this the week of Tyler's wedding."

Noah cringed around his bite of biscuit, and Ezra

slumped back against the cushions. "That cringe doesn't begin to cover it. Al let me have it, deservedly so, and it was a wake-up call. The first of a few I've had since."

"I'm sorry," Noah said as he repositioned himself, knee back on the cushion between them. "I didn't mean to pry."

He patted Noah's knee. "You deserve to know. You were a part of our family too. We missed you, but I'm glad you missed that part."

"But you and Mrs.—Al—came through it friends?"

Ezra smiled at the correction, smiled too at how well he and his ex had weathered the storm that had threatened their lives. "Splitting up was the only way we were going to save our friendship and the trust between us, bedrocks we couldn't afford to lose. We couldn't afford to lose each other either."

"Are you still—"

He cut himself off, biting the corner of his lip again as a blush crept up his neck. And finally they'd returned to the question Noah was still trying to figure out how to ask.

"Fucking each other?" Ezra offered and chuckled as Noah's blush raced higher and redder. "No. My workaholic tendencies weren't the only thing not working for us. Al is a Domme and an exhibitionist. She likes an audience. Her kink, not mine, but I was willing to make it work because she satisfied mine too. But I've gotten more private in my old age."

"About what? You're gorgeous." His eyes sprang wide again, and he stuffed the rest of the biscuit into his mouth, clearly trying to stop further truths from escaping.

Truths Ezra liked. "Good to know you think so," he said with a wink. "And no, it's nothing to do with being self-conscious. I just got tired of performing."

He finished chewing, then, hands clasped in his lap, he stared at them as he asked, "Performing?"

"For others. Like at the party you walked in on all those years ago. I'm at the point where I want to share those kinds of intimate moments more privately."

Noah lifted his gaze—bravery or curiosity Ezra couldn't say, but he'd take it. "What kink of yours did she satisfy?"

"I like to take orders. Sexually," he said, continuing to speak frankly, hoping the casual, matter-of-fact way he laid things out would make Noah comfortable, would encourage his curiosity, encourage him to be brave and ask more questions. Because there was no use hiding the ball or letting puritanical stigmas get in the way of his truth, not with someone he felt safe sharing that truth with. "I'm so used to giving orders in every other aspect of my life that not having to do so during sex sometimes frees space up here." He tapped his temple. "It's how I can get out of my head for a bit and enjoy myself. Sometimes I need to give someone else control."

"So in the kitchen a couple weeks ago..."

Under Noah's definitely curious stare, Ezra's own cheeks heated. "Yeah, the command in your voice got to me. Not every command will, there's more to it than that, obviously. But it's been a while, I trust you, and the evening was already charged, at least for me, and you're—"

"I'm what?" Curious morphed into brave, Noah holding his gaze. Into bold as he scooted closer, shin pressed the length of Ezra's thigh, a hand laid atop it, an arm stretched behind Ezra across the top of the cushions.

Ezra stared at Noah's shin, at his hand, struggling to bring to mind Band-Aids and sandcastles. "You're Tyler's childhood best friend."

"I'm not a child anymore."

"No, you're not." The hand on his thigh was large, the fingers long, a dusting of hair on the back of the palm. More than a dusting on the well-defined shin pressed against his thigh. What would that hair feel like beneath his fingertips? How thick or thin would it be in other places? How would it feel against his tongue?

What about the erection making itself known behind the zipper of Noah's shorts? In a bold move of his own, Ezra lifted his gaze and met the heated gray one only inches away. "You're gorgeous too."

"So if I told you to kiss me right now?"

"You don't have to order me to kiss you. You just have to ask."

"Can I kiss you?"

Ezra cupped the side of his neck, thumb skimming the edge of his beard, the coarse hair tickling, tempting. "Yes, Noah Becker, you can kiss me." He guided Noah's lips closer and felt the other man's smile land against his, felt Noah's first tentative brush of lips, his relieved exhale, then the boldness take hold, Noah firmly pressing their mouths together, his tongue tracing the seam of Ezra's lips, asking for entrance. Ezra granted it, opening for him and whimpering around his tongue when it swept inside, all the night's flavors magnified by Noah's own unique taste, by the strength of his long fingers digging into Ezra's thigh and the warmth of his other big hand sliding around his opposite shoulder and curling Ezra closer.

"Fuck," Noah groaned. "You taste good."

"That's all you." He skated a hand up Noah's back and relished the reflexive shiver. "All that wonderful food you made for me. All my favorites."

"You needed it." He edged the hand on Ezra's thigh higher, notching it in his groin as he pressed his front along the length of Ezra's side. "You feel good too."

The contrasts—Noah's gentle strength, his smooth lips and wiry beard, the earlier shyness that had evaporated—were making Ezra crave more than food. He pushed back against Noah's arm, slumping into the cushions, and before Noah could panic that he was pulling away, Ezra used the hand still around his neck to pull him along too. "You can feel more of me."

"Fuck, yeah," Noah said, picking up on where Ezra meant for him to go. He planted the knee already on the cushion, rose, and swung his other knee across Ezra, straddling his hips and stretching all that glorious torso above Ezra's.

Ezra coasted his hands over Noah's pecs, the heat through his tee searing. "My God, you're fucking beautiful." He dragged his nails over Noah's nipples that pebbled under the cotton. "And responsive."

"I've got a sexy ginger beneath me. I'm horny is what I am." He slammed their mouths back together, plowing his hands into Ezra's hair, sliding them down his neck, then over his chest, returning the teasing torture. Ezra glided his own down Noah's back to his waist, then up the front of his thighs, the hair there deliciously ticklish beneath his fingers. He shoved under the hem of Noah's cargo shorts, under the edge of his boxer briefs, far enough to grab the underside of his quads and urge him lower, in desperate need of friction.

Noah grazed the stiff ridge of his cock and groaned. "Oh fuck, is that—"

Ezra nipped his earlobe. "You know damn well what that is. That's all you too. All for you." And just like that, Noah became putty in his arms, the heavy weight of his chest draping across Ezra's, his taint riding the length of Ezra's erection, and his stiff cock digging into Ezra's belly. "That's it, Noah." He thrust up. "Feel all of me, then tell me what to do with this."

"Keep doing what you're doing." He ground down and drove his tongue back inside Ezra's mouth, giving Ezra all the friction he needed and more. Sliding a hand over his hip, Ezra grasped an ass cheek and held on tight, held him closer, as they rutted together, climbed higher and faster, as they chased—

George Michael's "Faith" filled the room, blaring from Ezra's phone vibrating on the side table. As good as ice water, Noah jerked back, clearly recognizing the ring tone Ezra had never changed, even after musical ring tones fell out of favor. He couldn't bear to part with one of his favorite musicians or from the song that had been at the top of the charts the day his son was born.

"I should go," Noah said as he scrambled off Ezra's lap, gaze averted, and began pitching empty food containers back into the tote.

By the time Ezra silenced the ringer and texted Tyler that he'd call him back, Noah was almost at the door. Ezra raced to get there first, slipping between Noah and the plank of wood. "Thank you for dinner tonight."

He looked anywhere but at Ezra. "Just returning the favor."

"No, you weren't." Ezra cupped his cheek and drew Noah's stormy gaze back to his. "Let me take you to dinner this weekend."

"Like a date?"

Ezra smiled. "Like a date. I'll tell you more about what I need. Maybe it's what you need too. I think you'd be a natural." Heat flooded Noah's eyes, but that divot was back between them, something worrying him, holding him back. "Don't overthink it, Noah. I'm just here for the semester. It doesn't have to be a thing. We'll see if we're compatible in bed, and if we are, we share some intimate moments and delicious meals while I'm here." He nibbled at his bottom lip, a good sign. Ezra pulled it free with his thumb. "We already trust each other. Let's enjoy each other too. Get out of our heads a little together. Either way, we part reconnected." It wasn't playing fair, but he drew Noah in for another kiss, lingering until the corners of Noah's mouth ticked up. "Is that a yes?" Ezra asked as he drew back.

Noah smirked. "You know it is." He slung the strap of the tote over his shoulder. "I'm off Sunday. There's a place up in Wilmington I've been wanting to try. Driftwood. They use one of our same purveyors but higher end. Eight-ish?"

Sounded like the perfect place with the perfect company. "It's a date."

Chapter Nine

"You smell like you took a bath in cocoa butter."

Abel's assessment wasn't wrong. "I'm trying not to wind up a lobster again," Ezra replied as he stood from his boat seat and reeled in some line. It was a lovely day, not a cloud in the sky, the sun bright and gleaming off the gentle waves that rose to meet the Carolina-blue horizon. Perfect for a fisherman like Abel who'd spent half his life on the water, a recipe for disaster for a pale New Yorker who'd spent half his life in an office. Did it soothe his soul? Yes. Did it soothe any physical part of him? Absolutely not. And he had hopes for the physical later. "I have a date tomorrow night, and I'd like to enjoy it."

Abel propped a foot on the boat's rail and let more of his line go. "What's this now?"

"Don't act like you don't know. You were the chief of police and visit Blue Plate at least twice a week. I'm sure the gossip's made it your way."

He smirked but kept his eyes on the water. "Noah's a good kid."

"Oy, don't say that." He shoved his rod back in the holder and plopped into the seat. "He's thirty-three."

"Only meant it in the colloquial sense."

"Yeah, like he's a kid compared to us."

Abel shrugged. "Didn't stop me marrying Rachel."

"How did you get past it?"

Abel's coal-black gaze swung his direction, twinkling with mirth.

Ezra rolled his own eyes. "Okay, yes, she's beautiful, but I know you better than that. There had to be more."

Mirth turned to genuine affection. "So much more. So much good, in her and for me. Age didn't matter."

Ezra propped both feet on the rail and hung his arms over his bent knees, watching their lines bob in the water far more gently than the thoughts bouncing around in his head. Was it really the twenty-five-year age difference between him and Noah that was keeping him up at night? No, he and Al had played with younger people before. Hell, six months ago he'd fucked a twentysomething bartender in a coat closet at a charity event. But he hadn't built sandcastles with any of those people. While Ezra could ignore—almost forget—the past in the heat of the present, in the aftermath, in his bed alone at night, staring at the ceiling, his memories returned. As did the doubts and recriminations about what he was doing in the present. "You knew Rachel when she was younger, right?"

"I did."

"That's the part I'm struggling with. Reconciling the

Noah from a decade ago with the man I had across my lap the other night."

Abel adjusted his line once more, then put the pole back in the holder and turned in his seat, reaching into the cooler between them and pulling out two bottles of water. He handed one to Ezra, then settled back in his seat. Ezra waited. He'd known Abel for going on thirty years, and patience while the giant gathered his thoughts and words was usually rewarded. Today was no exception, Abel settling back in his seat, angled his direction. "I did know Rachel as a kid. Worked with her too at the station. Seeing the person she'd become, I knew she was good to the core, right here." He tapped the bottle against his chest. "And that's the type of person I wanted to be around. Wanted to share what life I got left with."

Ezra ran a nail through the bottle's paper label. "Did it change all of a sudden or over time?"

"Bit of both. After my brother-in-law and nephew died, I had to take over at the station, but I was cut up too like the rest of the family. Mitch had been my best friend all my life, and Cal was like a son." His voice cracked, and he blinked rapidly a few times. Ezra reached out, a hand on his shoulder. Abel patted it with his, then shifted back toward the water, briefly checking his rod before taking a slug of water. He was steadier when he spoke again. "Rachel made sure I kept going. That I ate, that I slept, that I had everything I needed to keep working till we nailed their killer. Then she gave me someplace—someone—safe I could fall apart with because I didn't want to put that on the family I had left."

"I'm sure they would've been there for you."

"I needed to be there for them. Rachel was there for me. And I fell for her, hook, line, and sinker. When I almost lost her last year..."

"That Shakespeare case?"

He nodded. "Didn't matter how young she was or that I remembered the first time I took her and my niece out on this boat together, she was it for me." His smile was wide as he spun the wedding ring around his finger. "Loving that woman is the best thing that ever happened to me."

Ezra's chest warmed, full of happiness for his friend who'd walked alone for too long. "You're one of the good ones, Abel. Always have been."

"You're one of the good ones too." He smiled and jutted his chin at the rods, Abel's starting to bow like maybe there was something on it, Ezra's dangling suspiciously free. "Even if you can't fish worth a shit. Hope Noah doesn't expect you to catch his dinner for him."

"No, thank God. We're going out to a restaurant up in Wilmington."

Abel stood, offered a hand up to Ezra, then began reeling in his line, little by little. "You two got a lot in common, and he's a good man. Quiet, smart, works hard, and is kind. And he sure can cook." He grinned over his shoulder. "Not sure you could do much better."

Ezra smacked his shoulder. "Hey!"

Abel kicked his shin, then hoisted a mackerel out of the water, grinning wide. "He couldn't do much better either."

Chapter Ten

"I'm sorry," Noah said as he balled up the tinfoil his greasy, delicious burger had come in. "I know this wasn't the date you expected." Getting a reservation at Driftwood had taken longer than anticipated, that date set for next Sunday now, which was how he and Ezra had ended up on the beach, eating takeout from Pier Point, Hanover's favorite dive bar by the water.

"No apologies necessary." Ezra popped the last bite of his double cheeseburger into his mouth and hummed contentedly. "We would have had to reschedule anyway now that I have that emergency winery meeting tonight. And I have zero complaints about a juicy burger, a charming beach picnic, and more time with you."

"I don't get an adjective?"

"Too many to choose from."

"Cheater," Noah said with a smirk.

And got Ezra licking his fingers clean for it. Cheater indeed. He tossed his foil into the bag as if he hadn't just shamelessly put ideas in Noah's head that neither of them could do a damn thing about tonight. In some ways, though, it had made the date tonight easier, less weighted down with expectations, more about sharing each other's company and getting to know each other better. "You know the only thing that would make that burger better?" Ezra said.

"What's that?"

"Your chili."

Noah laughed and shook his head. "Absolutely not."

"Why's that? Your chili was amazing."

"I know. It's what got me the job at Blue Plate."

"I don't doubt it." Ezra tilted toward him, an arm braced behind Noah's back, a bent knee resting on his thigh. Easy, casual touches that warmed Noah's soul and made the blood running through his body simmer. "So why's it not good enough for a burger?"

"I didn't say that."

"Explain the logic," he said, borrowing one of Candice's favorite phrases.

So he did, explaining how the Texan chef he worked with in Richmond would argue what Noah made wasn't chili at all since it had beans in it and how any Tar Heel would argue it had no place on a hot dog or hamburger either. The "chili" for those, at least in North Carolina, he'd learned, was a fine ground beef simmered low and slow with ketchup, onion, cider vinegar, and other spices. Sweeter and saucier than the chunky-style chili he served at Blue Plate. He finished his verbal vomit and face-palmed, two-handed, and groaned behind his fingers. "I can't believe I just spent ten minutes of a date with a hot guy explaining hot dog chili."

Ezra leaned closer. "A hot guy who asked, who loves food almost as much as you do, and who is happy to spend ten minutes with you period."

All of that sounded wonderful...and unbelievable. Noah peeked out from behind one hand. "Why?"

"Why what?"

"Why me?"

Ezra waggled his brows and bumped his side. "Did you miss the beautiful guy part on my couch earlier this week?"

No, he hadn't missed it, hadn't forgotten a minute of that night. How could he? He'd mentally replayed it countless times as he'd tried to wrap his head around everything that had happened at Ezra's apartment.

All that Ezra had told him—about the Rosins, about the changes in his life, about what he needed in the bedroom.

All that Noah had felt—the joy of sharing a meal, the comfort of being around someone who knew his secrets, the simmering interest in Ezra's desires, the heat that had boiled over when their lips had met and Ezra had pulled him onto his lap. Deep kisses, greedy hands, a hard body below his... and fuck, now was not the time for a boner.

Gentle hands circled his wrists and drew them down, Ezra holding his hands. "I like you, Noah, and this, spending time with you, calms me, which is what this sabbatical is all about. You pulled me out of a spiral and kept me from falling back into it. I like me when I'm with you. Might be the first time I've liked me in a while."

Noah squeezed his hands. "You're too hard on yourself."

"Only what I deserve." He kissed Noah's knuckles. "I also feel safe with you, which as Archer reminded me, we don't find everywhere and with everyone. It's a gift."

Guilt whispered at the back of Noah's mind—was he actually putting Ezra in danger?—but his heart shouted louder, beyond grateful he could give back a little of the safety Ezra had given him. "I feel the same with you, now and back then. That night thirteen years ago was the worst of my life, but it wasn't all bad."

"How's that?"

"That's the night I realized I wasn't alone. That there were people in my life who I admired who were successful and who were also queer. Knowing that was possible, it kept me going all these years, brought me here." Using Ezra's hands still in his, he drew him the rest of the way forward into a kiss. "To you again."

"Full circle."

"Something like that." He stole one more kiss before standing and holding out a hand for Ezra. "And I want to know more about the other parts of that night. About what you need."

"You don't have—"

Noah tugged him into his body, slinging an arm around his waist. "I know. But I want to try. I want to give you that safe space too if I can."

Ezra coasted fingers over his beard, along his jaw, and Noah wanted to purr, to wallow in the bubble of warmth he'd never let himself get too comfortable in before, to consider the future he'd never let himself dream of. A safe space with someone who knew all of him.

Ezra pressed their foreheads together. "Why me?" he asked, turning Noah's earlier question around on him.

Noah's answer was likewise a reflection, a similar truth they shared. "I like me when I'm with you too."

Chapter Eleven

"Looks like a space there." Noah pointed out Ezra's windshield at the lone open spot in the restaurant's tiny, packed parking lot. "Guess we know why it took an extra week to get a reservation." An extra week, it turned out, that Noah had needed to shop for a sport coat.

"I needed the week for grading and office hours," Ezra said over the whir of the convertible top closing. "And to sort things at the winery. Also didn't mind getting back into the Blue Plate rotation." He winked. "And seeing more of your aprons. Daily laughs are good."

"What was your favorite?"

"Probably *I like pig butts, and I cannot lie.*"

He chuckled and shoved Ezra's shoulder. "I meant the food."

"Shrimp and grits," he answered around a smile. "And I'm judging that against Dram's version. You could give Greg a run for his money."

Noah doubted that, but just being mentioned in the

same sentence as the Beard Award winner was an honor. "Thank you," he said with a smile as he peered out the window at the Southern colonial home that had been converted into a restaurant. "I hope this place lives up to the hype."

"They've done a nice job from the look of it. The bright white paint with the black doors and windows. All those accordion windows pushed open. Gives it a modern, breezy feel."

"They basically gutted the place," Noah said, recalling the article he'd read about it. "They could have gone traditional, but I'm guessing they were going for less stuffy."

"Agree." Ezra reached for the door handle. "Let's go see what the inside looks like." His excitement was contagious, reminding Noah of those evenings when he and Mrs. R. would come home from a new place they'd tried, and Ezra would spend at least an hour regaling them with the highlights. Noah had missed experiencing Ezra's excitement over the years. He held on to that thought, that feeling, and pushed back the apprehension that had tiptoed up his spine as the week progressed, lodged in his brain heading into tonight. Would this meal conjure up the bad memories from the past too, the truth of what he'd been running from? Would tonight lead him to conclude that his old life in New York was one he'd completely left behind? That he should leave Ezra in the past too? He hoped like hell not—the closeness and safety continuing to bloom between him and Ezra was addictive—but good things had rarely lasted in his life. Hell, they only had a semester with each other as it was. Part of him knew it would be easier—safer—to walk away now, but that was the last thing he wanted. He'd done that before. Yes, it had saved him from his father, but how much of his soul had it killed in the process?

His door opened, snapping him out of his thoughts. "Hey, where'd you go?" Ezra said as he stooped down to meet Noah's eyes.

Away, was on the tip of Noah's tongue, a memory of similar eyes and a similar voice just beneath the surface. But that night had been one with little hope. Tonight, hope was definitely on the menu. Hope for all sorts of things, a good meal to start. The good kind of excitement.

"I'm right here," he said, sliding his hand into Ezra's waiting one.

As they meandered up the walkway to the house, Noah took the time to admire his date in the soft glow cast by the porch lights. Ezra's sunburn was finally settling into a tan, his copper hair was getting longer, curling over his ears, and the dark jeans and black jacket over a crisp dove-gray button-down, open at the collar, were what fantasies were made of. As if the professor attire all week hadn't been fantasy fodder enough. All Ezra's clothes fit him like a glove, obviously tailored, and Noah fiddled with his over-long jacket sleeves, trying to look at least halfway presentable.

Ezra stopped them shy of the front steps, covering Noah's fidgeting hands with one of his. "Stop drawing my attention to these." He lifted his gaze, eyeing Noah through his lashes, the look in his blue eyes unmistakable.

"You'll make me want to get back in the car and go straight home so you can put them to better use."

"That doesn't sound half—"

Ezra cut him off with a kiss, brief but delicious. "I said stop."

"It's not a bad idea." Noah looped an arm around his waist, drawing Ezra closer, pressing them together from chest to knee. No mistaking either what Ezra's presence and sharp appearance were doing to him. And he wouldn't be the only one noticing. "You walk in there, looking as good as you do tonight, and I might have some competition."

Ezra palmed his ass under the tails of his sport coat. "I'm not planning to date anyone else while I'm here."

"But this is casual." Gaze averted, he toyed with a few of the red and silver hairs at the open collar of Ezra's shirt. "And if I can't give you what you need—"

Ezra cupped his cheek, drawing his gaze back up. "Yes, this is only for the semester, but I'm only interested in you while I'm here." He scooted closer, notching his denim-clad cock—also hard—next to Noah's. "And if this is any indication, orders or no, I think we'll still have a good time."

Noah muffled a groan, then stepped away before he really did drag Ezra back to the car. He clasped his hand and started toward the steps. "We should go in now or else we're not going to make it through those doors."

"You should know I was tested before I left New York. Negative. And there's been no one since."

Noah nearly missed a step. Despite all that had happened in Ezra's apartment last week, despite the fact they were here on a date, Ezra's statement made it clear where he intended this night—the next few months—to go. Made it very real.

Made hope flare in Noah's chest. "Negative too. And it's been a while."

Ezra winked. "Won't hold that against you."

The front door opened, saving Noah from a witty reply that would surely lack wit. "Welcome to Driftwood," the host greeted. Dressed in slacks and a button-down, sleeves rolled up, his smile warm and welcoming, he was the picture of Southern hospitality, though his accent spoke of somewhere deeper south than North Carolina. "Do you have a reservation?"

"Under Becker," Noah said. "Table for two."

"Perfect. We have a table ready for you upstairs." As the host led them farther inside, Noah immediately understood why reservations were hard to come by. The tables at the two windows on either side of the front door were two of five in each room, ten total tables on the lower floor, each placed far enough apart to be private. "How many tables do you have?" Noah asked as they climbed the stairs.

"Nineteen, sir, counting the private dining room." He gestured to the room on the left at the top of the stairs, then led them into a larger room to the right, four cantilevered doors open, two- and four-tops split between them, two six-tops in the middle, and three tables in a wide arch around the fireplace in the far corner. "We pride ourselves on giving each table a unique experience and our guests our full attention." A black-and-white-aproned server stood beside the two-top in the far window bay. "I'll leave you in Mario's capable hands."

They thanked the host, then Ezra stepped forward, hand outstretched. "I'm Ezra," he said, shaking Mario's hand. "And this is my date, Noah."

Noah appreciated the directness. No mistaking him as Ezra's son, and no homophobes wanted here. Mario's kind smile was encouraging. Noah shook his hand next. "We look forward to working with you."

Mario's grin widened as Noah had hoped. It was a turn of phrase he'd heard occasionally, something else he appreciated, diners who liked to collaborate, who engaged, who didn't just view restaurant staff as there to take their orders and sling their food.

"First time dining with us?" Mario asked as they settled at the table, claiming perpendicular sides, Ezra scooting his chair closer to the corner and him.

"Yes," Noah replied. "Though I also work with your charcutier."

"You know Peter?" Mario said.

"I'm the cook at Blue Plate in—"

"Hanover!" Mario all but shouted, then nodded an apology to the other nearby patrons and lowered his voice. "Chef and I were there a few Sundays ago when we were in town checking out purveyors." Noah's day off, the reason he didn't recognize him. "Great stuff. Our diners rave about it too."

Ezra leaned close and stretched an arm over the back of Noah's chair. "He's being modest. He's more than just a cook. He's been chef'ing since he was seven."

Noah's cheeks heated as his gaze collided with Ezra's affectionate one. "I hardly call toad in a hole chef'ing."

"It was more than Tyler could do." He shifted his attention back to Mario. "My son could barely pour cereal into a bowl. His best friend here could operate the stovetop."

Mischief, the good kind, twinkled in Mario's eyes. No judgment there. "Well, we'll be sure to put our best foot forward. You'll want to start with charcuterie?"

"Please," Noah said.

"I have a marvelous Franciacorta that would go perfectly with the board tonight."

"We'll take two glasses," Ezra said. "Thank you."

"I'll bring over some water too and let you get familiar with the rest of the menu."

Mario bustled away, and Ezra leaned back in his seat, arm still draped over Noah's. "This building alone was worth the visit."

"They carried the brightness inside." Noah ran his hand over the smooth acacia tabletop. "Modern, but"—he pointed at the reclaimed wood ceiling beams—"they've kept a good bit of the old too."

"I hope we can do half as good a job renovating the winery."

"Tell me more about what you've got planned."

Ezra spent the next few minutes filling him in on the latest developments at the winery—how their plans to make the operation biodiverse and the facility energy efficient had won points at last week's meeting, how the unusual varietals that thrilled Archer were going to take some additional maintenance and erosion control to satisfy the county, how some minor seating capacity changes to the farm-to-table restaurant he and Tyler planned to open on-site were enough to win approvals for the prized dining permits, the other reason he'd bought in Sonoma County versus Napa County, food permits for wineries virtually impossible in the latter.

None of it sounded easy. "And this is your retirement plan?"

"Little secret," Ezra said as he crooked his finger, beckoning Noah to lean closer. "I don't know how to retire."

Noah laughed out loud. "That I believe."

He bumped his shoulder. "It is more time in the fresh air and closer to Ty and Sloan, who will inherit it someday. It's something I can give them—a real legacy—versus just another company that I buy and sell."

Before Noah could ask why the dip in Ezra's smile, Mario reappeared with a bottle of Ca' del Bosco and an impressive charcuterie tray. He poured the sparkling wine while detailing each of the meats and cheeses on the board. "I'll let you two enjoy, then be back to take the rest of your order in a little bit if that's all right?"

"Perfect," Noah said. "Thank you."

"You were right," Ezra said once Mario was out of earshot. "The later reservation was a good call."

Noah was pleased too that it was working out the way he liked, the staff relaxed and friendly, in no hurry to shoo them out the door and turn the table over. This didn't seem the sort of place to do that, regardless, which was another point in the win column.

Ezra lifted his glass for a toast. "Cheers. To getting out of our heads for the night."

Noah clinked his glass against Ezra's and sipped at the delightfully fresh and active sparkler, even as Ezra's words reminded him of the questions that had been nagging him. That if they were being direct with each other, if this evening was going where Ezra had indicated on the way in, he needed the answers to. "How..." he started but wasn't sure which question to ask first. He took another sip, then tried again. "How does it work? For you?"

"Not just for me," Ezra said as he lowered his glass. "For me and a partner. For us if you're interested."

Noah nodded. "What exactly does 'orders' entail?"

"That scene you walked in on all those years ago, Al was orchestrating every part of it." He leaned closer and lowered his voice. "Telling me when and how to play with his nipples, how to suck his cock, when I could touch my own. Making it so I didn't have to think, so I could just enjoy the moment we were in." Noah gulped, and Ezra chuckled as he kissed the hinge of his jaw. "That's advanced stuff. We can start slow, you guiding me through masturbation, some delayed gratification, you telling me how to suck your cock. What you like." He slid a hand over Noah's thigh under the table, not pressing for more, just warm and comforting, a connection. Noah had to bite his lip all the same, suppressing a groan. It was cute how Ezra tried and failed to hide his pleased smile before continuing. "But before all that, we talk and set ground rules. Limits and safe words. *If* you want to do it at all." He slid his hand higher, achingly closer to where Noah's erection was back. "I'm happy to stick with kissing and making out for now."

"I want more of that too." They'd stolen kisses and teasing touches on the way back from the beach last weekend and as they'd crossed paths in Blue Plate during the week, but time had not been on their side. Until tonight, and he wanted Ezra to enjoy all of it, dinner and after. "But I'd also like to try the other. To give you what you need. I'm just..." His words died, caught behind the other big worry he had about this whole thing. It grated that the root cause was the same as the worry he'd expressed to Candice when he'd first learned Ezra was in Hanover.

Ezra gently squeezed his thigh. "But what?"

"I'm worried about going too far given my dad's tendencies."

Anger flashed in Ezra's gaze, the blue hard as ice. Noah had only seen that look on his face once before—when he'd dropped him off at Penn Station that night thirteen years ago. Once the surprise had worn off, the fury had built, and before Noah had gotten out of the car that night, he'd had to extract a promise from Ezra not to go after his father. Tyler and Al couldn't lose him too. Some of that anger clearly still lingered. "Your dad was controlling to the point of abusive. Was physically abusive. Granted, I haven't been in your life for over a decade, but nothing I've seen so far and none of your friends lead me to believe you're anything like him."

He wove his fingers through Ezra's still on his thigh, staring at their entwined hands, his callused one larger and tan, Ezra's freckled and refined. "I don't want to hurt anyone, including you."

"And that's what'll stop you." With his other hand, he lifted Noah's chin, drawing his gaze back to a much calmer blue one. "And I will too. Trust runs both ways. You have to trust I'll tell you when I've reached my limit. And I have to trust you'll stop."

"But we haven't known each other for thirteen years."

"Which is why we start slowly. Build trust." He unlaced their hands and shifted toward the table. "For starters, I hate blue cheese. Tell me what to eat, but the blue is past my limit."

"Tell you—"

"Give me an order, Noah."

The desire in Ezra's voice, the edge of excitement, pushed Noah's worries some of the way back. Far enough to give this a try. "Take the crostini, a dab of stone ground, the wild boar, and the P'tit Basque."

He did exactly as instructed, eyes fluttering closed as he bit through the stack. "Delicious," he purred, and Noah didn't think he only meant the charcuterie. They continued on in that manner, Noah enjoying bites as well, until only the blue was left on the board.

"Not a fan?" Mario said as he swung by to top off their glasses.

"I'll get to it," Noah said. "Can we get a little honey? And do you have bread or crackers with walnut?"

"You are good. I'll be right back."

"Are you going to ask me to eat it? Tempting me with a better pairing?" Tempting was Ezra's low husky voice as if each bite he'd eaten were gravel. That voice, combined with the obvious pleasure he'd taken from the food and the orders, had made Noah hard as a rock.

"No," he croaked out around the desire that was riding him hard. He slid a hand over Ezra's thigh, squeezing more rough than gentle. "Those accompaniments are for me. I won't ask you to go past your limit."

Ezra tangled their fingers, then slid Noah's hand up, directly over the ridge straining behind his zipper, trusting him more. "Thank you."

Chapter Twelve

Dinner was exceptional, the service too. His and Noah's first impressions of Driftwood had been correct. Nothing about the place was stuffy. The food was elevated without being pretentious. The wine list tailored to the menu; quality without busting the budget. The servers and chefs were generous with their time and smiles, many of them making a trip out to introduce themselves. More than a few who Noah did recognize from Blue Plate. By the end of the meal, when it was only their table remaining, the chef-slash-owner and Mario, a married couple it turned out, had joined them at the table for a whiskey that had turned into an hour-long conversation about their inspirations for the restaurant and the renovations.

Any worries Ezra had had about the evening, about spending the rest of the semester enjoying his time in Hanover with Noah—enjoying Noah—were banished by the end of it. Sure, there were similarities to the past, but the present was far evolved from it—sharing an amazing meal with Noah instead of only telling him about it, working with talented chefs and servers who clearly considered Noah an equal, letting Noah order and order him, trusting his food and wine choices and trusting he'd respect Ezra's limits. He'd done beautifully, in the pairings and the directing, and Ezra, as a result, had been hard since that first bite of cheese.

And almost came in his jeans like a teenager when Noah crowded close behind him at his apartment door and wrapped his arms around his waist, his dick nestled against Ezra's ass, his lips peppering his neck with open-mouthed kisses. Ezra bobbled his keys. "Your food and wine picks tonight were spot on," he said, trying to focus on anything but Noah's wandering hands. "Just like your flavors at the diner."

Noah nipped the crook of his neck. "Thank you, but if you want me to pick where this"—he lowered a hand and cupped Ezra's stiff cock through his jeans—"goes tonight, then you need to open the damn door."

He jutted his hips forward and angled his neck, giving Noah better access, idly wondering if Noah could feel how hot he was for him all over. He rocked his hips back. "You feel so good."

"Will feel even better when we're naked and sweaty."

Yes, that was an eventuality Ezra could get behind. He righted his head and smirked over his shoulder. "Fine, you win." Properly incentivized, he got the key in the hole, turned the knob, and pushed open the door, then was pushed inside by the sexy chef at his back, who with one spin was at his front, kicking closed the door and wedging him up against it. "Is someone being a sore winner?" Ezra teased.

Noah shoved his dick against Ezra's hip. "I'm sore all right."

He took hold of his jacket lapels and yanked them apart and down, ridding Ezra of the garment. He stepped closer, stretching his big body the length of Ezra's, and Ezra groaned, hooking a leg around his thigh, making sure Noah didn't go anywhere. "What are you gonna do about it?"

"Claim my prize." He tunneled his long, strong fingers into Ezra's hair, tipped his face just so, then brought his lips down in a fierce, devouring kiss. He licked, nipped, came up for air, then dove in again, his kiss a dish Ezra could easily fill up on. But Ezra wanted more than just the tasty appetizer tonight.

He drew back and sucked in air, shivering with sensation as Noah trailed his hands lower, down his neck and to his shirt collar. He worked free the buttons and slid his hands under the material, fingers splayed, pinching his nipples before traveling higher...and freezing.

Oy!

Noah's worried gray eyes shot to his. "Oy?" His fingers lightly traced the scar they'd stumbled upon. "Ezra, what happened? Was this my dad?"

He winced, not from any pain but at the wobble in Noah's voice, the edge of fear he'd never wanted to hear there again. "No, no, no." He gently clasped his wrists and gave them a light squeeze, enough to bring Noah back to the present with him. "One more bit of news I need to catch you up on." A headline that Ezra had dragged his feet sharing, afraid it would send Noah running, the reality of Ezra's age and workaholic lifestyle made neon bright. No help for it now.

"Do we need to sit down for this?" Noah asked.

Smiling, Ezra rocked his hips, rutting gently, stoking the embers between them, not wanting the fire to burn out before it had really gotten started. "I'm comfy right here."

"I wasn't sure—"

"You remember how I talked about a wakeup call."

"Tyler's wedding."

"That wasn't rock bottom." He released Noah's hands and finished removing his shirt, fully exposing the two-inch scar just above his left pec.

Noah ran his fingers over the raised skin and gulped. "A heart attack?"

"Not exactly. Stress-induced arrhythmia. I basically fried the wiring. My heart rate couldn't regulate and that led to some fainting spells and a very panicked Al who thought I was going to die right there in row C of the Richard Rodgers Theatre." *Worst birthday present ever,* she chided him still, and he let her because he'd never forget the stark fear in his fearless best friend's eyes before his world had gone black. If Al needed to find humor in the memory in order to live with it, so be it. Same reason he'd let Ty rail at him for ignoring his health and didn't protest whenever his son asked about his next cardiology appointment. "I needed new wiring in the form of a pacemaker."

"Fuck, Ezra." Noah pitched forward, resting his forehead on Ezra's shoulder. "If you'd..."

Ezra carded his fingers through his loose top strands. "Shh, don't go there."

"You wouldn't be here. We wouldn't have reconnected. I wouldn't have gotten the chance to show you what a difference you all made." He raised his head, and his eyes were glassy, his voice wavering to match. "To say thank you."

Ezra stifled the objection, the calming words, the self-recriminations. This was how Noah needed to work through the news. Ezra had to let him have it, same as he let Al and Tyler cope in their own ways. He cupped Noah's cheek, wiping away a stray tear. "You're welcome."

Noah nuzzled into his palm, breathing deep, pulling himself back together. "I'm sorry about the scare, but I'm glad it wasn't him." He released a long, slow breath, relief perhaps, then returned his gaze and fingers to the scar, back in the present with him. "This is the other reason for the life changes?"

He nodded. "Trying to reduce stress and enjoy myself." He lifted Noah's face with a crooked finger beneath his chin. "And this has been a very enjoyable night so far. I'm not ready for it to end."

"Are you sure—"

Ezra firmed his grip and infused his voice with as much conviction and confidence as the quiet moment would allow. "Don't treat me like fine china. Think of me like a vintage Mustang." He thumped his chest. "One with a brand-new engine that'll run another thirty or forty years."

Noah laughed more fully, humor reaching all the way

to his eyes along with renewed heat. He stretched over Ezra again, forearms propped against the door on either side of his head, mouth close enough to feel the breath of his words. "A Mustang, huh?" He clasped the underside of Ezra's leg still hitched around his thigh and used it to haul him up and into his arms, deliciously crushed between the hard door and his hard body. "You buck like one too?" he asked, voice rough and full of gravel.

Ezra flicked out his tongue, teasing the crease of his lips. "Only one way to find out."

Chapter Thirteen

Noah lost his shirt somewhere in the hallway, Ezra yanking it off over his head, as he continued making his way to the bedroom. He kissed along Ezra's collarbone, the lingering scents of dinner mixing with his sandalwood body wash. Fucking intoxicating.

But not nearly as intoxicating as his words. "I have some ideas that involve you in the chair in the corner of my bedroom, ordering me to undress, then making me edge myself until you're ready to stick your cock down my throat and make us both come."

Noah stumbled, spun, and fell back against the bedroom doorjamb.

Ezra smirked. "Would you like that, Noah?"

Both hands on his ass, Noah held him tight and rocked his hips, showing him just how much he did. "One edit. You'll come with your cock down my throat too." The sexy man in his arms groaned and whined and shimmied his hips for more friction. "Would you like that, Ezra?"

He draped both arms over Noah's shoulders and kissed a path from his ear to his lips. "You're a tough negotiator."

Noah laughed between kisses. "Says the retired corporate shark." He pushed off the wall and walked the rest of the way into the bedroom, only letting Ezra down once they were beside the bed.

And then froze, heat creeping up his chest and neck, a wave of nerves hitting him hard. They'd talked about this, had practiced a little over dinner, but actually doing what Ezra suggested, trusting himself not to go too far...

Ezra lifted a hand and cupped his cheek. "You don't have—"

"I liked it at dinner." He snaked an arm around Ezra's waist. "I want to give you what you need." He ducked his chin. "I'm still learning to trust myself, I guess."

"Trust me. And if at any time you want to stop the scene, say squash blossoms."

A surprise laugh escaped. "Squash blossoms?"

"First thing that came to mind." Smiling, he stepped closer and kissed the underside of his chin. "You did beautifully at dinner. I don't doubt you will here too."

"What are the limits?" Noah asked. The blue cheese one at dinner was helpful. Gave him some boundaries to work within. He needed those again.

"Light spanking is fine, but I'm a hard pass on anything harder."

"I wouldn't—"

He put his fingers over his lips. "I know *you* wouldn't. But these are limits I give anyone I play with. My pain tolerance isn't high, six out of ten. For any bondage scenes,

I'm claustrophobic enough I have to be able to see the door. And no humiliation. That takes me out of the scene completely. And when the scene is over, I like to be held."

Hold him, Noah could do that. Would love to all night long. As for the rest of it, his head was spinning. He was queer but kink was new territory. At least Ezra's limits were ones he didn't see himself bumping up against.

"Limits for you?" Ezra asked.

"I don't know," he confessed. "I've never done this before."

"Trust me, then. I'll be watching and listening for your tells, and 'squash blossom' if you need it. That's what safe words are for." He smiled and aimed Noah toward the chair. "Now go sit and tell me what to do."

Trust. If Noah was going to do this, he needed to give some of that back to Ezra. Trust all that he was with Ezra. Trust that he could maintain his cool while giving Ezra what he needed. He stopped in front of the chair, took a moment to tie his hair up and toe off his socks and shoes, then dropped his own jeans and boxers. He grabbed the blanket off the back of the chair, spread it over the seat, then turned.

And met his first test in restraint. Ezra's gaze was fire, the blaze sweeping Noah from top to toe, while at the same time a flush rose on Ezra's chest, bleeding all the way up his neck and cheeks. "Are you trying to make me come before we barely get started?"

Noah lowered himself into the chair, legs spread, not hiding a thing. "I'm trusting you and leveling the playing field some."

"And turning me the fuck on."

"You weren't already?"

"I've been hard since that first bite of cheese, but fuck, Noah, you're hotter than in my wildest dreams."

Noah dipped his chin again and smiled, the frank regard pleasing, making his own cock stiffen further. He gave it a stroke, delighted at Ezra's gasp, then withdrew his hand and forced them both to the armrests. "Ditch your shoes and socks and climb onto the bed." Ezra moved to unbutton his pants, and Noah clicked his tongue against his teeth. "No, leave them on for now." Ezra obeyed, kicking off his socks and shoes, then knee-walking onto the bed to wait in the middle for the next directive. "Pull the comforter down and prop yourself against the headboard. Legs spread so I can see how much you want me."

He chuffed and flicked his gaze down. "You can't tell that already?"

"I'll be able to tell a lot more once you get your hand down your pants."

Ezra hopped to it, resting back against the padded headboard, knees propped and legs spread like he'd been told. "Good," Noah praised and noted Ezra's answering smile, sweet and peaceful. He liked that. So did Noah's cock, pulsing, a bead of precome leaking out the tip.

Ezra licked his lips.

"Soon, baby," Noah said. "Unfasten your jeans and reach your hand inside your boxers. Let me see how you stroke yourself."

He fumbled once, then got the button undone and the zipper down. He shoved a hand inside mint green boxers visible through the open fly. "You weren't lying, were you?"

His hand moved under the fabric, stroking slowly, and he bowed off the headboard. "Not lying," he gasped. "Was imagining us back here. Like this."

"Just tonight? Or is this how you've been imagining me all week?"

He groaned and let his legs fall open wider. "Since we made out that night."

Noah dropped a hand to his inner thigh, and Ezra jerked his head back up, gaze following where Noah trailed his fingers. "Push your jeans down some and pull your dick out. Show me, Ezra. Let me see what I've been dreaming about for weeks."

His hand shifted under his cock, and then with the other, Ezra pushed his jeans and boxers down so he could pull out his cock and balls, glistening with precome. And fuck if Noah's mouth didn't go dry, if he didn't almost bolt out of the chair to fall on his own knees and shove his face in the copper hair at the root. He wanted to smell, he wanted to lick, he wanted to taste. He let his head fall back as he wrapped a hand around his own length and stroked. "Fuck, Ezra, maybe I should have left my pants on."

"No, baby, I'm enjoying the show too."

Noah righted his head and found Ezra stroking himself with one hand and pinching his nipple with the other. "Leave your cock there and play with both your nipples. Show me what you like but don't hurt yourself."

Eyes still locked on Noah's, he lifted the hand that had

been around his dick to his mouth and shoved three fingers between his lips.

"Holy fuck," Noah cursed, hips rocking up. "Is that what you're going to do to my cock?"

Ezra smiled around the fingers, removed them from his mouth, then swiped the moisture over one then the other nipple, playing with the wet nubs that wrinkled and hardened under his touch.

His cock bobbed, wanting attention, and fuck if Noah could stay seated any longer. "Can I come to you?" he asked.

Ezra nodded as he keened, and Noah shot out of the chair and across the room, onto the bed and between Ezra's spread legs. "Keep your hands right there. Close your eyes and tip your head back, tweak your nipples while you imagine me spreading your thighs"—he pushed them apart —"and swallowing your dick." He bent over and took Ezra all the way to the back of his throat.

Ezra bowed his back and thrust up his hips. "Fuck!"

Noah flicked his gaze up, pleased to see the rest of Ezra following orders, pleased to see all that freckled skin flushed with desire, writhing for what Noah was able to give him. Noah worked Ezra's cock with his fist and mouth, an alternating rhythm of slow wet glides up and down the length, flicks of his tongue around the head, twists of his hand around the base, fingers teasing the curls there, bringing him right to the begging edge before he pulled off.

And Ezra stayed right where Noah had ordered him, legs spread, head thrown back, fingers working his nipples, albeit more gently now, following that order too.

"Fuck, you're marvelous. Look at me, Ezra. Look at how worked up you've made me too." He righted his head, and Noah moaned at the evidence of his own work. Blown-wide pupils, barely any blue left, a bottom lip made more plump by the teeth that had dug into it, hair tousled from where his head had tossed and turned against the padded headboard. "You are hands down the most beautiful man I've ever seen." There was so much he wanted to taste, to touch, but judging by Ezra's heaving breaths and the weight of his own balls, they didn't have much longer this round. "Remove your pants and boxers but keep your eyes on me."

Proving turnabout was fair play, Noah shoved three of his own fingers into his mouth, sucked, and chuckled a little around them when Ezra's pant leg got caught around his ankles.

He glared playfully. "I have an equally beautiful man distracting me."

Noah removed his fingers. "Since you're on your side, stay there." He finished ridding Ezra of his clothes, then holding a leg up, teased his taint with his wet fingers.

Ezra tipped his torso forward, hands fisting the sheets, groaning into the pillows. "Noah, please."

Noah continued to run slick fingers over his perineum while rutting his slick cock against the ass cheek in the air. "You asked for edging." He circled Ezra's hole and ached at the shiver it produced. "Trust me, this is edging both of us."

"Need to come with you."

Noah pressed a finger in. "How do you want to do that?"

"Your edit," Ezra panted as he rode back on the finger. "Please."

"How flexible are you?"

He twisted his torso, almost to where his back was flat, while Noah thrust another finger inside him. "Fucking yoga finally pays off."

Noah laughed out loud, then nearly choked when Ezra's tongue flicked the tip of his dick. "You want that?"

"All the way down my throat."

His balls drew up tight, and he hissed through his teeth. "I'll be lucky to make it two thrusts."

"I'll be lucky to make it one."

Noah smiled. "We better hurry, then." He repositioned on his side facing Ezra, a forearm in the mattress near his groin, the other arm still thrown over his hip, pushing three fingers back inside Ezra's hole as he buried his face back where he wanted to live for the foreseeable future, nestled in copper curls with his mouth full of cock, Ezra's scent strong, his precome salty, his desire on the edge of bursting.

Ezra's hot mouth closed around Noah's dick, tongue circling the head and flicking the slit before licking all the way to the root, and Noah groaned from deep inside his chest, the whole of him rumbling, vibrating.

And Ezra spilled, filling Noah's mouth and senses with lust and relief, filling his heart and mind with trust and comfort. Two thrusts later, Noah came undone, out of his head, in the safety of the arms of the person who'd always protected him.

Chapter Fourteen

Noah moseyed over to Ezra's side, the both of them watching as Candice sank another stripe into the nearest corner pocket. Annie, her cheerleader while Kari and Jaylen were at the bar, clapped from across the table. But Noah only had eyes for Ezra's easy, sexy smile. "Thank you for coming out with us tonight."

"The whole town is here." He gestured around the packed interior of Pearl's, the twenty-four-hour sports bar and pool hall next door to Blue Plate, hopping after an HU football win over their conference rival. "And so are you." He smooched Noah's cheek. "No place I'd rather be."

"Cat's out of the bag, though," Candice said as she rounded the end of the pool table. Noah figured she was referring to him and Ezra. This was technically their first date night out in Hanover, but Ezra's daily presence at Blue Plate the past three weeks, plus Holly's gossip grapevine, should have already spoiled that news. Or maybe Candice was referring to something else, her smirk devilish as she bent and lined up her shot at the eight ball. "Now you know how terrible he is at pool." She took the shot. Sank it.

Annie hooted. "And rack 'em!"

Noah held his pool cue out to a laughing Ezra. "Why don't you play Candice?"

Ezra pushed the cue back his direction. "Not if I want to keep my winning streak alive. She's beat half this bar already."

"Hustling pool was how I got off the street," Candice told him as Noah emptied the table pockets and rearranged the balls in the rack. It was a story he'd heard her tell before at the shelter. A cautionary one but also one of hope and happily ever after. "Was also how I met the birthday girl." She winked at Kari, who sauntered back their direction, Jaylen on her heels with a tray of shots.

"Birthday girl would like a round of shots with family and friends," Kari said. "Then a dance with her wife."

Noah snuck a glance at Ezra, pleased to see him so effortlessly blending in, so effortlessly everything. Confident, sexy, smart. Relaxed. Noah liked to think maybe he'd played a hand in that last one over the past few weeks, Ezra slaying his sabbatical goal with each passing day.

Each day that brought him closer to the end of it. That brought them closer to the end of their time together.

Noah shook off the thought and raised his glass. Tonight was for celebrating, about enjoying a night out with his friends and Professor Sexy. He hid is satisfied grin from no one, and Candice rolled her eyes as she handed her cue to Ezra. "See if you can do any better teaching him." Then she disappeared into the game-day crowd with Kari, Jaylen, and Annie, the happy couples on their way to the dance floor.

"I'm guessing pool was not how you supplemented your trust fund," Ezra said as he lined up behind the cue ball, preparing to break.

"I never touched it."

Ezra missed the cue ball completely, then rocketed back to standing. "But the attorney should have been able—"

"I asked him not to." Noah closed the distance between them and laid a hand on his hip. "Before I left that night, my dad said if I ever touched a dime of it, he'd come and get the rest of it. Hell, he tried to take it all when I didn't, but he couldn't without my consent or a court order."

"He looked for you," Ezra said, putting it together. "So the ten years between when you left and came here, you were on the run?"

He nodded. "He sent PIs looking for me. Hated me, said I was a disgrace, but he hated that Mom had left me that money more. He almost caught up to me the first couple of moves. I learned not to get comfortable after that."

Game forgotten, Ezra laid his cue on the table, then hoisted himself onto the table rail. "Did you think about letting him have it?"

"Never." And not because he wanted it for himself one day. "It would have killed my mom. That was her family money. Her legacy."

"What did you do, then?" Ezra tugged him closer, into the vee of his legs. "If you want to tell me…"

"Hopped between shelters. Would offer to help in the kitchens. Learned everything I could. I was in one in Maine when a chef with a catering business dropped some food off one day. Worked for him for a while until he wanted more than I could give." One of the cautionary tales he'd told the kids at the shelter. Ezra tugged him closer still, and Noah let that less than fond memory fade away in the safety of the present cocoon. "Had to leave there, but I landed a dishwasher gig in Philly. It was a hole-in-the-wall place in a shit part of town but good people and good food. I've been in restaurants ever since."

"And working your way up." Ezra's smile was full of pride and zero pity. Noah breathed a sigh of relief. "Any further PI sightings?"

"Not since I've been here."

"Are you planning to stay?"

Noah's gaze strayed in the direction of the dance floor, to the best boss and friends he'd had in thirteen years.

Ezra pressed a hand to the center of his chest. "You don't know how at this point, do you?"

"I don't want him to use anyone to get to me."

"For what it's worth, Al filed a TRO against him, and he never came at us again. He moved out of the building six months later."

Another relieved breath. "I'm glad you didn't have to deal with him anymore."

Ezra tapped his hip, waited for Noah to step back, then hopped off the rail. He grabbed their cues, handed Noah his, and lined up again behind the cue ball. The strike was perfect, scattering balls across the table. "So where to next?"

None went into the pockets, though, and Noah circled the table, considering which shot would embarrass him least. "I never quite know. Just somewhere close to the water."

"Could I tempt you to Sonoma? I need a chef, and you're a good one." Ezra waggled his brows, but it wasn't enough to unstick Noah from where he'd frozen half-bent over the table. "Don't look so panicked, babe." Ezra closed the distance between them and ran a hand over his back. "We can fuck then go on to being great business partners. Look at me and Archer."

Noah ignored the pinch in his chest caused by Ezra's words and focused on the practical problems with Ezra's proposal instead. "I don't know anything about cooking that sort of food." He took a shot and missed completely, the cue ball hitting nothing but rails.

"I wouldn't want you to cook that sort of food." Ezra missed his shot on a stripe. "We're on a misty mountainside overlooking the coast. On the rare day you can see through the fog. I want cozy comfort food in a cozy, comfortable setting where folks can enjoy good wine, good food, and the ones they love." He leaned into Noah's side. "A place where we're all safe."

"Sounds like heaven."

"It does, doesn't it?" There was nothing casual in Ezra's gaze, nothing that said they would just be business partners if Noah came with him to California. The tension in Noah's chest eased, a smile spreading across his face that Ezra reflected. "I tell you what," he said, turning away from Noah and back to the table. "Each ball I sink, you tell me what dish you'd put on the menu."

"I can't just—"

"Yes, you can." He bent, aimed, and sank the five.

"Coq au vin."

Ezra raised a brow.

"Or pot roast if it makes you feel better. In either case, it's perfect for soaking up alcohol, goes with any red, and it's warm. Perfectly cozy."

"All right." He crossed behind Noah, a hand trailing across his back, sending shivers up Noah's spine. Another shiver raced behind it as he sank the two ball.

"Veggie pot pie."

"Yes!" Ezra said, smiling wide. "Those are amazing." As was his shot to sink the one.

"Chicken and dumplings."

Pocketed the three.

"She-crab soup."

"With Dungeness?"

"Not if I can help it."

He laughed out loud, drawing admiring looks from the women a table over. On the way to line up a shot on the six, Noah clasped his shirt and hauled him in for a brief hard kiss. "Fennel citrus salad. That was a freebie."

Or not, as Ezra sank both the six and seven in one shot.

"Lamb sliders."

"Two more," Ezra said. "Give me an app and a dessert." The four found the corner pocket.

"Calabrian chicken wings."

Ezra grinned once more as he passed behind him, his hand drifting lower, squeezing. "For all the marbles, baby."

"I think I've been hustled."

Ezra feigned surprise, a hand splayed on his chest. "I have no idea what you're talking about."

Noah laughed. "Shoot your damn eight ball."

Eight ball, side pocket, clean.

"Peach cobbler in the summer. Apple cherry galette in the winter."

Ezra raised his arms. "You're hired."

Noah stepped into his arms, pressed against the confident, sexy man he couldn't get enough of, who was sketching out a dream Noah wanted to believe. "Don't tempt me."

Ezra's lips ghosted over his. "Maybe I want to."

Chapter Fifteen

Ezra followed his nose to the kitchen and found an increasingly familiar, always welcome sight—Noah in front of his stove on a Sunday morning, cooking up something delicious. Looking equally delicious. The menu had changed with the season, well into butternut squash and other fall vegetables now, and Noah's morning attire had changed too, the funny aprons and running shorts traded for sweatpants and fitted tees. Ezra had zero complaints about any of it—Noah coming to his place after work on Saturdays with his overnight bag, spending the rest of the weekend together, a parting breakfast at Blue Plate on Monday morning. And though a good chunk of their time had been spent together the past weeks, Ezra was ahead with his classes and Noah was cooking lights out, in Ezra's kitchen and at Blue Plate.

Like the bacon and butternut squash hash Ezra spied from around his shoulder. "Is this going to be on the winery menu?"

"Sunday brunch."

He liked the sound of that. Liked all the warm skin under Noah's thin white tee as he coasted his hands up Noah's toned delts and around to his front, hugging him from behind. "Is Candice wondering who your new muse is?"

He stirred the hash in the cast iron skillet with one hand and flipped an egg in the fry pan with the other. "Candice is smart. I don't think she has to wonder too much."

He kissed the back of Noah's shoulder. "What gave me away?"

"Oh, I don't know, maybe it was us making out at Pearl's later that night or the day you grabbed me by the front of the apron from across the counter and laid one on me." The smile in Noah's voice brought the same to Ezra's face.

"Well, the first was due to you laying out a sexy as fuck menu, and as for the second, the original Professor Sexy was in town. I had to make sure he knew that you"—he grabbed one of Noah's ass cheeks—"had been claimed by the new Professor Sexy."

"Is that what you were doing?" He flipped off the burners, and in the next blink, Ezra found himself on the kitchen island, legs spread, his boyfr—Noah—standing between them. "Claiming me?"

Ezra leaned back, arms braced behind him, fingers curling around either edge of the island. Dick tenting the front of his flannel pants, Noah's gaze fixated on exactly what Ezra wanted *him* to claim. "Aren't you doing the same?"

Noah was a split second from making good, his hands curled into the waistband of Ezra's flannels, when three sharp raps sounded on the door. "Go away," he shouted. "I've got my hands full of the new, better Professor Sexy."

Ezra laughed out loud. "Better. I like the sound of that!" He leaned forward, kissed the smiling man between his legs, then lay farther back on his elbows, stretching and lifting his hips, arching the way Noah liked and making it easier for him to slide the bottoms free. Warm hands slid under his cheeks, saving them from the cold granite, holding his cock right where—

Three knocks against the door again.

"Fuck," Noah cursed, his warm breath coasting over Ezra's cock, making him shiver and ache.

"Get rid of them." His voice came out a needy plea, and Ezra didn't have it in him to be embarrassed. He just wanted to be fucked.

Noah shifted, appeared at his side, his cheeks flushed, his pupils blown wide, almost blotting out the gray. "When I come back, I'm gonna order you to jack yourself good and slow until you're writhing all over this island, then I'm going to eat you for breakfast, starting with your hole and ending with your cock."

"Fuck." Definitely a whine. He shot a hand down, angling for his balls, or maybe just one stroke of his cock, anything to stave off his orgasm.

Noah flicked it away. "No touching until I'm back."

Ezra curled his fingers around the edge of the island again, Noah's orders easy to follow.

The knocking started again.

"Oy!" Noah shouted. "I'm coming, or rather my boyfriend and I were about to if someone wasn't knocking down our damn door."

Everything about the uncharacteristic gripe warmed Ezra's insides. The *oy*, the *boyfriend*, the *our*. While Ezra's brain was fighting all evidence of reality, his heart and Noah's words were far closer to the truth of what they'd been doing—becoming—the past six weeks. With that acknowledgment, whether intentional or not, the sort of peace Ezra usually felt under a lover's orders washed over him. He eased his grip on the counter's edge, flattened his back and ass against the cool granite, and breathed deep, floating on the calm warmth.

Until a familiar voice floated around the corner from the foyer. "Boyfriend? You're a bit young for my dad, but I'm sure you gave him a good—" Tyler's words cut off about the time Ezra found his pants. "Hudson, is that you?"

Fuck! He shoved his legs into the flannel pants, then stumbled around the corner and into Noah's back. His entire frame was rigid, his entire being subtly vibrating, and when Ezra rounded his front, Noah's gray eyes swirled with fear... and longing. Ezra remained close as he turned to face his son. Ty stood on the welcome mat, hands on his denim-clad hips beneath the hem of his Dram branded hoodie. "Ty, what are you doing here?"

He dragged his disbelieving gaze from Noah and turned a confused, betrayed one on Ezra. "I finally got a meeting with that chef in Raleigh. Thought I'd swing down for a visit."

"But Sloan—"

"Couldn't wait to get me out of her hair." He ran a shaky hand through his own red locks, disrupting his usual coif. "Mom's back from LA and helping out. She was supposed to call you."

He winced, remembering the calls from Al he'd ignored last night.

"Didn't expect to find you shacked up with my best friend."

"Noah lives in another unit here at the complex."

"He said *our* do—who's Noah?"

Ezra moved from Noah's front to his side and gently clasped his hand, prying open the fist and weaving their fingers together. "Tyler, this is Noah Becker. Noah, this is my son, Tyler."

The divot between Ty's eyes deepened. "But he's—"

"Not the same kid who bled all over your 'Vette thirteen years ago," Noah said before shifting toward Ezra and dropping a kiss on his forehead. He squeezed his hand, then slipped his own free. "Goodbye, Ezra."

He grabbed his wallet and keys out of the bowl on the entry table, slipped his feet into his running shoes, and disappeared out the door.

Ezra couldn't help but feel like he'd just slipped out of his life too.

For good.

Chapter Sixteen

Ezra took two minutes to clean up in the bathroom and throw on jeans and a sweatshirt before returning to the kitchen to find his son pouring champagne into a flute. "Bit early, isn't it?"

Tyler's blue eyes cut to his. "Clothed is an improvement." He opened the fridge, pulled out the orange juice, and topped off his glass. "This is not an improvement, but one decency for another."

Ezra pulled his son into a sideways hug. "Since when are you a prude?"

"Since I walked in on my former best friend and my dad about to have sex."

Ezra flicked his gaze to the counter beside them. "Right there."

"Oh God, stop," Ty groaned. "What a shanda." He pushed out of Ezra's arms and bolted out of the kitchen, taking refuge in one of the kitchen chairs. A sip later, he lifted his gaze and Ezra's good-hearted, earnest son was staring back at him. "That *was* Hudson, right?"

Ezra tapped his chest. "Here, yes. Same heart, same goodness." He turned to the stove and assessed the egg as a cold goner, but the butternut squash hash was warm enough to salvage. He split it between the two plates Noah had set out, then carried them over to the table. "Same talent here too." He returned to the kitchen for silverware, the champagne bottle, and another glass. Fuck the orange juice. "Noah Becker is an incredible chef who left Hudson Selby behind the night I dropped him off at Penn Station."

"Has he been here in Hanover the entire time?"

Ezra shook his head. "Only the last few years."

"And before that?" Tyler asked between greedy bites.

"In kitchens, up and down the East Coast."

They spent the next several minutes enjoying Noah's food, Ezra filling Tyler in on the dish and some of the other standouts Noah had cooked for him, and Tyler filling him in on the chef in Raleigh. An okay fit for a future project, but not the wow factor Ty was looking for. Which apparently he'd found with Noah's food.

"This"—he gestured at the last bite of his hash—"is the food you need to be serving at the winery. It's hearty and comforting while also complex and everything Wine Country loves. It's perfect for those fog-shrouded hills."

Ezra would be lying if he claimed his own mind hadn't drifted to the idea almost daily since that night at Pearl's, how it had materialized in almost perfect clarity with *oy, boyfriend,* and *our* less than twenty minutes ago. How it had shattered when Noah had walked out.

"Why didn't he reach out?" Tyler asked. The softness of his voice, the wobble betraying the faux outrage, exposed the same longing Ezra had seen in Noah's eyes.

Ezra finished his last bite, lowered his fork, and topped off their glasses, the real difficult part of this conversation upon them. "He didn't want his dad to find him."

"He can't think we would have—"

Ezra laid a hand over his. "He was protecting *us*, Tyler. It was never about protecting himself. Not then, not since, and not now."

Tyler ran his other hand through his hair, flattening the coif completely. "Did you find out he was here? Come here to find him? Feel guilty about not knowing? Because I still don't get it."

"Don't get what?"

"Any of it."

Ezra squeezed his hand. "My poor baby boy. Is your head exploding?"

"Yes," he admitted before downing the rest of his champagne.

"This is when we need Sloan."

"And Mom."

One last top-off and Ezra slumped back in his chair. "I came here because I needed to chill the fuck out."

Tyler cocked a brow. "Chill the fuck out? How much time have you been spending with Hudson?"

"Noah, and I think we can thank my students for chill the fuck out. But it's no less true. I needed to downshift. That was never going to happen in New York. And it wasn't going to happen if I dove right into running the winery. I needed a break."

"And it has been? A break?"

"Mostly." He smiled around a sip. "I spiraled around the time of the first exam, but Noah brought me out of it. And to your question, no, I didn't know he was here. That was a happy accident."

"And this thing with Hud—" He paused, swallowed hard, then after a nod, restarted. "This thing with Noah, is it just a break?"

"That's what we agreed to."

"Not what I asked." He tipped his glass toward the foyer. "And not what he said when he came to your door."

His son was as shrewd, if not more so, than he and Al combined, but he also had a pretty face and smile that could charm the dollars and truth out of anyone. "His life is here, for now at least. He's got good people around him and a great job. He's safe here if he chooses to believe that. My life is about to be across the country, and whether we like it or not, there is an increased chance of his father finding him if he stays with me."

"Are you sure he doesn't want some of his old life back?"

"Maybe." He shrugged. "The good parts. But like I said, he doesn't want to risk our safety for it. I guarantee he's at his place panicking because he didn't want you, Al, or anyone from his old life to know where he was."

Tyler averted his gaze, trying and failing to hide the wetness gathering in the corners. "He renamed himself Noah, my middle name."

"Don't be angry with him."

"I'm not angry." He sniffled as he twirled the stem of the empty wine glass. "I married a victim of abuse. I get it as much as I can. He did what he had to do for safety. I'm just sad we missed all this time with him. He was part of our family too."

"He couldn't reach out, but he remembered us." He shifted out of his chair and crouched next to his son, a hand on his shoulder. "He remembered his best friend the only way he could."

"I just... I missed him." A tear escaped, and Ezra drew Ty into his arms, holding him tight. For as popular as Ty had always been, the number of people he had truly opened up to and kept close was a much smaller circle, and for a long time, that had been only Noah. "You think he's gonna bolt again?"

"Maybe," Ezra said, then not wanting to lie to his son, wanting him to be prepared for the sting of pain ahead, admitted "Probably."

"Do we need to go stop him?"

"It has to be his choice, Tyler. We have to give him time." Time had worked in Ezra's favor before where Noah was concerned. He just hoped it would work in his favor again. Soon. He didn't have much of it left in Hanover.

Chapter Seventeen

"I haven't seen you in here on a Sunday since you and Professor Sexy started doing the—"

Noah looked up from his notebook, and Candice's words died.

"That's why I called you," Alicia said from behind Candice at the prep table, working the Sunday brunch rush with Jordan.

Noah couldn't blame her for calling the boss. He'd slunk into the kitchen, grabbed his recipe notebook and a stool from under the prep table, and set up shop in the storeroom, as far out of the way as he could be, in the place he felt safest.

Candice seemed to sense that, not coming any closer. She crossed her arms and leaned a shoulder against the doorjamb. "What are you doing there?" She jutted her chin at the notebook.

He didn't want to see her flinch, to see her disappointment, so he went back to scribbling as he spoke. "Making sure you have all the recipes you need."

"You're leaving?"

"Soon."

"I knew it was coming, but I figured you'd leave at the end of the semester when Ezra did."

"That was the plan." Not originally. If Ezra hadn't shown up in Hanover, he would've left by mid-September, but he'd bought into enjoying himself, had forgotten about keeping the ones he lo—cared about—safe. He should have never compromised Candice's safety, the safety of everyone at Blue Plate, or Ezra's and Tyler's now too.

"Something spooked you," Candice correctly surmised.

"Tyler's here."

"Ezra's son?"

He nodded. "My former best friend."

"Can I come in there with you?"

Would he ever find another boss as good? Who understood him so well? Whose patience was seemingly endless? He took a deep breath and closed the notebook. He owed her more than he could ever repay, more than a notebook of recipes. "I can come out."

"No, you stay there." She grabbed a stool and brought it into the storeroom, setting up close but not crowding him, even in the tight space. "Did Ezra tell him you were here?"

He shook his head. "Tyler surprised him. Shock of his life, I imagine. Finding his dad and former best friend about to fuck on the kitchen counter."

"Not gonna lie, either one of you is a tasty snack."

Laughter bubbled out of him, and some of the fear and anxiety of the past hour escaped with it. A tiny bit of relief.

Candice rubbed a hand across his upper back. A tiny bit more. "Feel better?"

"A little."

"Why are you panicking?"

He propped his heels on the upper rung of the stool, rested his elbows on his knees, and hung his head in his hands, raking his fingers through his top strands. "I fooled myself into thinking Ezra and I were safe. I trusted he wouldn't say anything. We could stay under the radar and avoid my dad's attention. But with Tyler knowing now too..." He laced his hands behind his neck. "My dad's already hurt him once because of me. I can't let that happen again."

"Couple of facts to consider." She lifted a hand, index finger raised. "One, you can defend yourself—and them—now." Raised another. "Two, no one in this town is going to let anything happen to you, or to them, or to any of us. Don't you remember how everyone closed ranks around Charlie, Trevor, and Sean during their shit? They'll do the same for you and for Ezra and Tyler because they mean something to you and to Abel for that matter."

His brain knew she was right, but all his heart was telling him was that even more people were in the line of his father's vitriolic fire.

"Can I be real, Noah?"

He angled his face, side-eyeing his friend. "Do you know how to be anything else?"

"Nope," she said with an unashamed shrug. "How many years has it been since your dad's come looking for you? Since you've been in Hanover?"

"No," he admitted. "Since the stop before. Five years." He sighed and sat upright, took another deep breath, trying to convince his heart to believe her words. "You're right. He's likely given up by now. Said good riddance and made back whatever money he thought he'd lost. But it's so hard not to be afraid after all those years..."

She rubbed his back again. "You don't have to stay here, Noah. I'm just saying you can. That I think we'll all be all right if you do." She waggled her brows. "But we'll be all right if you go with Ezra too."

He chuckled and scrubbed his hands over his face, not wanting to admit how tempting that sounded. "If Tyler doesn't kill me first. I'm fucking his dad."

"Yes, Noah Becker is. Thirty-three years old, amazing cook."

He dropped his hands. "What if he hates me?"

"You never thought of this before?"

"I never thought I'd have to see him. I thought whatever Ezra and I are doing would be over at the end of the semester."

"*Thought*, as in past tense? Where are you in the present?" She didn't give him a chance to reply. She knew the truth as well as he did. She stood from her stool and pulled him into a hug. "No one hates you, Noah. Give Tyler a chance to get to know you, and I'm sure he'll understand why Ezra is with you if he doesn't already." She squeezed him tight. "And if all else fails, cook for him."

Chapter Eighteen

Noah gently scraped the sides of the mixing bowl with his spatula, nudging down the orange batter then folding it over the chocolate chips he'd sprinkled into the bowl.

Needs more chocolate, he recalled, a wisp of fond memory, and picked up the bag to add more chips.

The doors to the dining room swung open, and Holly bustled in. And bustled right over to him, swiping a chip from the stream he was jostling into the bowl. "Chocolate chip pancakes?"

"*Pumpkin* chocolate chip pancakes."

She popped the chocolate morsel into her mouth, then shrugged out of her coat, hanging it and her bag on one of the hooks by the door. "I've been working here as long as you have, and I've seen everything on the menu—all the usual favorites—but never these. Never *any* version of chocolate chip pancakes."

Because they were his best friend's favorite, and he'd

never been able to bear the thought of making them for anyone else.

"What's the occasion?" Holly asked.

The Post-it Note that had been in his overnight bag on his doorstep. The text he'd sent to the number on it. The return text he hadn't had the nerve to read.

"Thanksgiving treat," he lied.

She cocked a brow—she didn't believe him one bit—but she let it go and put on her apron. "There was an early bird outside. I went ahead and let him in. Totally under-dressed for this weather. Tourists," she muttered. "But he was a looker."

Noah left the mixing bowl on the prep table and peeked out the swinging door's small window. The answer to his text was sliding into a booth close to the kitchen, shivering in his jeans, button-down, and dark green corduroy jacket. His best friend was a looker—always had been—and he'd also been in California too long. That outfit was inadequate for winter anywhere else. But none of that mattered. Noah knew what that text message said now; Tyler had accepted his invite. He was there, and hopefully Candice was right. "He'll take a honey latte."

"Did he come in with you?" Holly gasped. "Are you stepping out on Professor Sexy?" Then she slapped his shoulder. "Please tell me you are not that stupid, even for Hottie Ginger."

He laughed, held a hand above the griddle to test the heat, judged it close enough, and tossed the ready hunk of butter onto the surface to melt. "Hottie Ginger is Professor Sexy's son. And an old friend."

"Ooh! Now there's a dish!" She covered her mouth with both hands, but it did nothing to hide the excited tittering behind her fingers. Excitement Noah needed to quash for all their sakes.

He lowered the heat and moved to the end of the island and gently clasped her wrists, lowering her hands but keeping them in his. "I know you're going to want to tell everyone in town about this, but this is one thing, Holly, that can't make the rounds. It's why I asked him to come in early."

All humor fled, the good woman Noah knew her to be staring back at him with nothing but heart. "This is important to you."

"He was my best friend, and I haven't seen him in thirteen years."

"Oh, Noah." She drew her hands from his and threw her arms around his waist, giving him a fierce hug. "Thank you for trusting me."

Noah returned the embrace. "Thank you for always being there for me." Point one for Candice. She was definitely right about his friends—his family—here in Hanover.

"I'll go get his latte," she said, stepping out of his arms. "You go tend to the griddle. Ten minutes or so?"

"Should do it."

She hustled out to the dining room and the espresso machine behind the counter, and when Noah emerged seven minutes later, Tyler had moved to the counter, and Holly was half-over it, sharing God only knew what stories.

"Let me guess," Noah said as he slid two plates of

pancakes onto the bar. "She told you about the great hollandaise disaster of 2021."

Tyler winked. "You're not the first chef to do battle with it."

Holly playfully glared Noah's direction. "I could have told him about the five-hour butternut squash soup that ended up on the floor." She straightened and hip-checked him out of the way. "Y'all have fun catching up."

"I put the extra batter in a muffin pan. Just pop it in the oven once it's preheated."

She twirled on her way back into the kitchen. "Love you, boss man."

Laughter helped breach what could have been an awkward couple of moments, just him and Tyler at the counter. "You want to go back to the booth?"

"I'm fine here if you are." At Noah's nod, Tyler picked up the syrup Holly had set out and drowned his pancakes in it.

Noah laughed. "Same ole sweet tooth."

"Don't tell my wife. There have been a few health scares lately, and she's gone full health nut."

"In a family full of foodies? How's that working out?"

"About like you'd expect." He shoved in a bite and did a happy dance in his seat. "And she's the worst cheat of all. The number of compound butters she has stashed in our fridges is criminal."

Sounded like Noah's kind of woman. "I've got a recipe for a citrus nasturtium one I'll give you before you leave."

"Thank you." He traded his fork for the coffee mug, hands cupped around it. "And thanks for meeting me."

Noah gestured outside at the first streaks of pink lighting the sky. "Thanks for getting up at the ass crack of dawn."

"I have small children. What is dawn?"

Noah chuckled. "Ezra said you had two."

"Yes, Hellion One and Hellion Two." He withdrew his phone from his pocket, swiped the screen to life, and two redheaded toddlers in plaid Chess tees smiled back at him. "They take after their mother."

"Not after you at all?"

"No comment."

Laughter flowed easily between them again, same as conversation had done the past few minutes, a miracle for all that had happened, all the time that had passed, but maybe that's what folks talked about when they said you could fall right back in with the best of friends like no time had passed at all. Noah had never let himself have that. Never gone back to visit the friends he'd made in this or that stop. Hell, he'd never stayed long enough—before Hanover—to make real friends. But none of them, he ventured, would come close to the one beside him. "I'm happy for you, Ty."

"You haven't lost your touch," he said around another bite of pancake. "I always knew this was where you belonged."

"In a small coastal town in North Carolina?"

Ty knocked his foot against the side of his shin. "In a kitchen, you goof."

His heart swelled at the easy camaraderie that pushed long overdue words to the tip of his tongue. "Listen, Ty—"

"I'm sorry."

"You're not the one—"

"No, please, let me say this." He set down his fork again, wiped off his hands, and angled toward him. "I never thought I'd get the chance to, and being with Sloan, who went through some of what you did, I should have done more, said something, been there for you."

"You *were* there for me." Noah reached out and covered his wringing hands. "How many times did you make an excuse for me to hang out at your place? Usually, the nights Dad was already halfway through a bottle. Or after we lost a race."

He cast his gaze aside and swallowed hard. "I should've stepped in before I did."

"Ty, look at me." Noah waited for him to lift his chin, to bring those bright blue eyes back to his. "At no time over the past thirteen years, or hell, even during all those years living across the hall, after Mom died, after Dad..." He paused to swallow down the lump in his own throat, memories closer to the surface than they'd been in years, cracking in his voice as he continued to speak. "At absolutely no time during any of it or after did I blame you or wish you'd stepped in sooner. If anything would've happened to you, I would have never forgiven myself. You stepped in exactly when you were supposed to, and before then, you and your family helped the best you could."

"Thank you." He flipped his hands, squeezing Noah's. "It's gonna take some time to process that guilt away but thank you."

Noah waited for him to return to eating his pancakes

before asking the question that had been niggling at the back of his mind, a worry he hadn't voiced to anyone yet, hadn't even been brave enough to admit to himself, that even the hint of it turned his stomach and hurt his heart—if it were true. He lowered his own fork, appetite gone. "Do you think that's what your dad is doing? Processing his guilt by being with me?"

Tyler nearly choked on his food, and Noah would have face-palmed if he wasn't busy slapping Tyler's back to dislodge the wrong-way bite. A guzzled drink of water later, Tyler had mostly recovered, though there was no help for his blush. "I assure you my dad is not fucking you because he feels guilty."

"I'm impressed you can say that with a straight face."

He flapped a hand in the air. "I've had a couple days to wrap my head around it."

"I've had several months, and I'm still not sure I have."

Tyler shrugged and went back to shoveling in the last bites of his pancakes. "Our family has never been conventional where love is concerned."

Noah dropped his fork but saved it from hitting the floor—where his stomach had dropped to—at the last second, even as his heart soared somewhere near the ceiling. "Love?" he croaked as he righted himself and found Tyler standing by his stool, two plane tickets in hand.

He set the first down on the counter. Wilmington to San Francisco. One-way. "For your future, whenever you decide to grab it, whether that's this weekend for Thanksgiving or a year from now. Pretty sure Dad wants you there with him, and he'll wait however long you need to be okay with that." He set the second on the counter. Wilmington to New York. Round-trip. "If you need to deal with the past in order to make that future happen." Both of them in the name of Noah Becker.

Noah shuffled them in his hands and brought hope forward, the SFO ticket on top. "And you'd be okay with this future too?" he asked Tyler.

"I'm better than okay with whatever future means I get to have my best friend back in my life."

Chapter Nineteen

The balcony doors slid open behind Ezra, and the peaceful San Francisco evening was filled with the happy sounds of children playing and the leftover aromas of turkey, stuffing, and all the fixings—a magnificent meal that had left Ezra stuffed to the brim.

But not too stuffed for mulled wine, the sweet spicy scents of cinnamon, cloves, allspice, and orange peel wafting from the mugs Al carried his direction. "Higher education agrees with you." She handed him a mug, then leaned a hip against the terrace wall where he stood. "It always did."

He sipped at the wine, warm comfort in a cup, letting it chase away the chill of the evening fog rolling in. "I've enjoyed it and the break from New York, but I wouldn't want to do it full-time."

"You want to go back to New York?"

"Fuck no. Why would I have bought a winery out here?"

She handed him her mug, then hopped up on the wide stone wall, her back to the Bay, the short gray curls of her new bob bouncing in the breeze. She made grabby hands for her mug, and the gesture was so like their granddaughter's that Ezra had to laugh. She nudged his belly with her painted toe. "Shut up and give me my wine." He caved but not without some teasing first, holding it out of her reach until she threatened to regale him with stories of fucking Archer all over his new winery. "Not that, please," he groaned as he handed her back the mug. He leaned against the wall beside her, watching the lights twinkle on the Bay Bridge. "We have friends who own vineyards and still live in New York," she said. "They fly out during harvest and run away from the snow during winter."

He turned the question around on her. "Do *you* want to go back to New York?"

And got the same answer. "Fuck no."

He chuckled. "That's what I thought."

She tilted his direction, bumping his shoulder. "I had to check. You're more relaxed, but something's on your mind. Has been all day."

More than just a day. It had been four days since Noah had walked out of his apartment, four since he'd spoken to or seen the man that had been in his life every day—in texts, at the diner, in his bed—for the past six weeks. Time and distance apart weren't making the ache in his heart or dick any easier to bear. He missed Noah more than he would miss a friend or a casual hookup. More than he was supposed to miss someone *he* was going to leave in a few short weeks. "I met someone."

Al hid her smile behind the rim of her mug, but there was no mistaking the twinkle of interest in her dark eyes. "The hot neighbor you were cooking dinner for a few months back?"

He nodded, then carefully tiptoed around the confidences he'd promised Noah. "He's Tyler's age."

"Even better!" She poked his side a little harder, and her smile widened a little farther. "Explains why you've avoided the barber. Gives your man something to grab on to."

"You're incorrigible." He playfully swatted her foot away, then ran a hand through his hair, remembering the last time Noah had done the same, thinking about how he wanted more of it, more of him. "I want him to come to Sonoma with me," he admitted, and that same sense of peace from Sunday washed over him. If only that were enough. "But it's not that simple." He set his mug down and rubbed his hands over his face, the warmth of his palms doing nothing to chase away the cold weary frustration that was settling in his heart and gut. "How can I ask him to leave his life behind for a shot with an old man and a risky business venture?"

Al gently clasped his wrists and tugged them down. "At our age, Ez, can we afford not to lay it all out there, to not take every shot we're given?"

He tipped his head back and sighed, the weight of the past week, of his tender heart, heavy. As clear an indication as any. "I think I'm falling for him."

"Oh, sweetie, I'm certain there's no 'think' about it." She looped one arm over his shoulders and drew him close, dropping a kiss on the crown of his head. "Tell him, Ez, what's here." She patted his chest. "And also consider what you're willing to give up or shift in your life to keep him."

The pensiveness in her voice gave him pause, a moment out of his own mire, and he stepped back, finding her dark eyes likewise mired in conflict. "We're not just talking about me, are we? Archer?"

"No, that was just some fun with an old friend." She tapped her short nails against the ceramic mug and turned her gaze to their grandchildren at the table on the other side of the sliding glass doors. "I was offered a secondment with a client."

"Al, that's great! You live for those assignments, getting to dig in with a single client as your sole focus."

"They're in New Orleans."

"And?"

She jutted her chin toward the house. "Our family is here in San Francisco now. The winery, the legacy we're building for our family, is ninety minutes up the road. What if this is where—"

He pushed off the wall, extracted the mug from her grasp, and set it beside his on the stone. He stepped between her legs and clasped her hands, holding them tight to his chest. "If you're gonna fly the nest, Al, you gotta actually spread those wings and fly."

She averted her gaze again, dark eyes on their fingers as they instinctively knitted together. "I haven't actually been on my own since I met you freshman year of college."

"And you won't be in New Orleans either. You'll be

chasing Amos around Dram while his daddies make out in the kitchen."

"Not a lie," she said with a chuckle. "And Greg and Tony are going to have even more corners to make out in with that second location."

"Which also means Tyler will be there more often, checking on his investment and getting it ready to open."

She rolled her eyes. "And because he just likes it there."

She wasn't wrong. New Orleans was firmly on the family circuit. "As do Sloan, and Miller and Clancy."

She smiled and squeezed his hands still in hers. "How did we go from only one son to having six kids?"

Because after they'd let one down, they'd each sworn never to make the same mistake again. Regret and guilt swirled in Al's eyes, the same person, the same memory on her mind as was on Ezra's. Except his guilt over the past had been assuaged, Noah convincing him otherwise with every dish he'd cooked and every kiss they'd shared. Now any guilt Al saw reflected in his eyes was over not telling his best friend the truth about the boy who'd lived across the hall and the beautiful man he'd become. The brilliant chef Ezra was in love with.

She released his hands and reclaimed her mug, handing Ezra's back to him as well. "Six kids, three grand-kids, and we're the ones talking about learning to fly for the first time?"

He held his mug out for a toast. "To later-in-life leaps."

The mug was barely to his lips when the glass door was thrown open hard enough to rattle and Ty came barreling out, white as a ghost. Al was off the wall in a flash, Ezra hot on her heels. "What's wrong? Is it Molly or Michael? Sloan?"

He shook his head, his blue eyes wide, locked on Ezra. "Noa—Hudson's dad."

Ezra froze, terror sluicing through his veins for the boy they'd all once loved, for the man he was in love with now. Had they failed him again?

He must have made some sound because Al's face whipped around, eyes catching his, then flashing with understanding. And in the next second, acceptance. She grabbed his hand, squeezed hard enough to ground him there, to keep him from giving in to the rising panic, before turning back to their son. "What about that asshole?" she hissed through her clenched teeth.

"He's dead."

Chapter Twenty

Noah reached the mouth of the inlet, rowed the shell into it, and as the rec area came into view, nearly dropped his oars. Ezra stood leaning against a dock piling, wrapped snug in a peacoat and scarf, the morning sun making his copper and silver curls shine. Noah's heart lightened for the first time since he'd received the call from his emancipation attorney. "You're free," he'd said. "For good."

It hadn't felt like freedom until now.

Until one look at the handsome man on the dock and the future Noah had held at bay for months crashed into him like a hurricane. Fuck, he hoped Tyler was right, hoped like hell Ezra wanted a future with him too because Noah could see it all, everything he hadn't let himself dream about for years.

He paddled the rest of the way into the small rec area and into the opening where the dock manager directed him. He made polite small talk as he checked in the rented gear even as his insides bubbled with anticipation. It was a wonder he didn't float the rest of the way down the dock to Ezra's side.

"Come with me," Ezra said when he eventually reached him. Noah slipped his hand into Ezra's and followed him back to his truck in the parking lot. Ezra lowered the tailgate, and the spread laid out at the end of the truck bed made Noah's insides fizz, made his heart float even higher. "It's been a while," Ezra said, "but I think I remembered what you need after a row."

He'd remembered everything by the look of it. Extra towels and dry athletic wear, a bottle of Gatorade and thermos of steaming beverage, and all the high-protein snacks he could want. Noah drew Ezra closer, nuzzling his cheek, drowning in the warmth and sandalwood scent he'd gone too long without. "I missed you."

Ezra sighed with relief as if he hadn't been sure of Noah's response. "I missed you too." He angled his face, a light brush of their lips, then drew back. "And we'll get into that in a few, but change first and get some food in you."

As much as Noah wanted to stay right there, to have the future conversation with Ezra now, his wet suit was cooling, and the dates and nuts were calling his name. "Don't go anywhere."

Ezra winked and boosted himself onto the tailgate. "I'll be right here."

Noah snagged the towels and clothes and moved to the side of the truck out of public view. He quickly dried and changed, then dumped the wet items into the backseat of his cab on his way back to Ezra and the waiting picnic. "Thank you for coming back early."

Ezra nodded and handed him a roll of turkey and cheese. "I wanted to be here for you."

Noah nibbled at the protein log and glanced toward the rec area where numerous one- and two-person boats were tied to moorings. "That's the first time I've been in a shell or held an oar in thirteen years." At first, he'd been convinced his dad would find out somehow, and then it had been too painful to remember the good parts of rowing. The days spent on the water with his best friend and the after-picnics the Rosins used to bring for him and Tyler. He'd been too afraid, too heartsore to row again, but there was a reason he'd always settled in places near the water.

"You're gonna hurt like hell tomorrow," Ezra said.

Noah reached for a date and winced. "Already do."

"Do you feel better, though?"

"My body, yes." Better than it did after any run, rowing second nature to him. Sure, he'd been the cox for most of his childhood—he hadn't had the body then for the other positions—but he'd practiced at all of them. Now, though, with strength he could only dream about having back then, he'd cut a path through the waterway with no trouble. Cutting through the thoughts and feelings rumbling around inside him, however, hadn't been as easy. "Here"— he tapped the side of his head, then his heart—"and here, are still a mixed bag."

Ezra angled toward him, knee folded on the tailgate, his other leg hanging off the end. "Talk to me."

"I was gonna go to New York. See if he'd changed, if

he'd recognize how I had, how I'd made something of myself."

"If it would be enough for him to accept you."

He set aside the handful of almonds, appetite waning.

Ezra reached for his hand, holding it in both of his. "Books and movies make it seem like a reunion and forgiveness is inevitable. But it's not. It's rare for estrangements to resolve. Al's parents died hating her for who she was and who she loved."

"Which is absurd. You're both wildly successful, respect each other, and have an amazing family."

He shrugged. "We're queer. That's all they could ever see." He left one hand in Noah's and snagged the thermos, taking a sip before handing it over to Noah. Hot cider, spiced with cinnamon and clove, eased gentle warmth back into his soul. "Do you want to go back for the funeral?"

"No, that part of my life is over now." He lifted Ezra's hand and kissed his knuckles. "I know the parts of it I want to keep."

Ezra's fingers tightened around his, and his eyes went molten, liquid ice, as bright blue as the sky above. "Do you mean that?"

"I do. I want to go to Sonoma with you."

Ezra grinned. "The winery chef job is yours. It has been since that night at Pearl's."

Bubbles again, threatening to escape and float him right across the tailgate into Ezra's arms.

"But if you want to stay here," Ezra said, "I get it. You have family here too—Candice, Holly, everyone in this town who adores you. I can make it work with trips out—"

Noah cut him off with three fingers to his lips. "They'll always be my family, and we can visit whenever we want, yeah?"

"Pretty sure Abel will demand it."

"And I can cook the same style food at the winery?"

Ezra tugged him off the tailgate and around to stand between his legs. "I want you with me in Sonoma, not only because I love you but because you are an amazing chef with exactly the right menu in mind already."

All that sounded amazing, but one part sounded beyond amazing. He loosened his hand and framed Ezra's face, the prickle of his scruff popping all those bubbles, sending fizzy warmth tumbling through him. "I love you too."

Their smiles collided in a languid kiss, no hurry to it, just love and safety and the promise of future and family ahead, one twenty-year-old Hudson couldn't have imagined in his wildest dreams. He leaned back enough to look into blue eyes that knew all of him. "When I said the good part about that night thirteen years ago was learning success was possible for someone like me, I had no idea it could look like this. A foggy hillside in Sonoma where all my dreams could come true with you."

"And you're good with that picture?"

He smiled as he nuzzled Ezra's cheek. "More than."

"You're a survivor, Noah. I admire *you*. I'm the lucky one who got to know you again, who gets to share our dreams and more together."

And more.

Noah chuckled, and Ezra brushed their noses together. "What are you laughing about?"

"Do you know what else I realized that night?"

"What?"

"That my best friend's dad was hot as hell. Never thought in my wildest dreams that he'd be on his knees for me one day."

"Oy!" Ezra nipped at his bottom lip. "Maybe you should take me home, then, and finish what you started on the kitchen counter."

Sounded like a dish—a life—Noah Becker couldn't wait to nosh on. He hauled Ezra off the tailgate, over his shoulder, and slapped his delicious ass. "Do you still have that sexy mesh underwear?"

"Not those, but I guarantee the blue pair on under these jeans are even sexier."

Oy! indeed.

Reviews are an invaluable tool when it comes to spreading the word about great reads. Please consider leaving an honest review for *Blue Plate Special* on your favorite review site.

Thank you for reading!

Acknowledgments

Third time's the charm! I'm so happy to finally bring you Noah and Ezra's story, which has been kicking around my hard drive for way too long. I'm also excited to restart the *Table for Two* series. There's a lot going on with the Rosins and their loved ones, so stay tuned for all the foodie shenanigans coming your way.

Many thanks to Cate Ashwood for the many covers on this one. I hope the sexy back was fun to work with in all its variations! Thanks as well to Kim for the beta read, formatting, and PA support, to Rachel for the beta notes and Yiddish consults, to Susie Selva for the editing advice that pulled this all together, and to Lori Parks for her keen and speedy proofing eyes.

Finally, thank you readers for hanging with me during the brief pauses from hackers, espionage, and mayhem. It's no secret I'm a major foodie, and these foodie romance stories are the palette cleansers I need every so often. Thanks for enjoying them too!

Also by Layla Reyne

For the most up-to-date list of titles and a helpful reading order, please visit www.laylareyne.com.

Agents Irish and Whiskey:

Single Malt

Cask Strength

Barrel Proof

Tequila Sunrise

Blended Whiskey

Angel's Share

Fog City:

Prince of Killers

King Slayer

A New Empire

Queen's Ransom

Silent Knight

Perfect Play:

Dead Draw

Bad Bishop

King Hunt

Best Play

Standalone Stories:
What We May Be
Under the Table

Table for Two:
The Last Drop
Blue Plate Special
Over a Barrel

Changing Lanes:
Relay
Medley
Freestyle

Soul to Find:
Icarus and the Devil
Jason and the Storm
Paris and the Reaper
Atlas and the Traitor

About the Author

Layla Reyne is the author of *What We May Be* and the *Agents Irish and Whiskey, Changing Lanes,* and *Table for Two* series. She writes sexy, intense LGBTQIA+ romance featuring competent adults in kitchens, sports arenas, car chases, and other high-stakes situations. Whether it's adrenaline-fueled suspense, rival athletes, vampires and shifters in alt-realms, or love mixed with mouth-watering foodie goodness, queer folks finding happily-ever-afters is guaranteed.

You can find Layla at laylareyne.com, in her reader group on Facebook—Layla's Lushes, and at the following sites:

facebook.com/laylareyne

instagram.com/laylareyne

bookbub.com/authors/layla-reyne

tiktok.com/@laylareyne

9 789898 692295 9